RIGHT NEXT DOOR

G. LOUISE BEARD

GLASSSPIDERPUBLISHING

Edited by Vince Font
Cover design by Judith S. Design & Creativity
www.judithsdesign.com
Published by Glass Spider Publishing
www.glassspiderpublishing.com

I have always enjoyed reading and spent my early years thinking that I wanted to be a writer, but the necessities of life delayed my dream. I eventually returned to the idea of writing after two years of retirement. There are many people to thank for helping me through the journey . . .

Sheryl, a most amazing young woman whose vision and insight helped me to press forward when the idea of writing was just resurfacing.

Sheila M, who listened to my words, made awesome suggestions, and gave very enthusiastic encouragement. She is the one who practically tied me to her kitchen table and encouraged (demanded) that I complete my application and mail off the stories disc. After we prayed together, she then went with me and stood as I mailed the package to Washington, D.C.

WS, my husband, my friend, my partner—the one who quietly watched and prayed for me as I sat day after day, week after week, and month after month developing the stories.

Mrs. Daisy Richardson, my mother, whose wise counsel kept me on track. Thank you, Mother, for believing I had the ability and for making me believe I could do it.

Tanoka (son #1, the engine), who never knew how his bright smile, soft kisses on the cheeks, and declarations of encouragement—"You're doing good, Mom, keep it going"—helped me to press forward through the times when I was floundering.

Darius (son #2, the caboose), who never knew how his great bear hugs and his soft-spoken words—"I know you can do it, Mom"—comforted me and helped me to continue on the journey.

To the Sisters of the Women of Prayer group: Thank you, ladies, for the laughs, the tears, and the praises that we share with and for one another.

Most of all, I want to thank God for His many, marvelous, and amazing blessings.

—G. Louise Beard

CHAPTER 1
Looking Back to Yesterday

It had been a long day, and Octavia was thankful to finally get home. All she could think of was getting out of her street clothes and into her swimsuit.

I didn't get a chance to do my laps this morning, she thought. *It's such a warm evening. I'm going to spend an hour in that pool and then get some of my new ideas on paper.*

It was important for Octavia to get her daily exercise; she was determined to keep her weight down.

It felt good to be released from the bondage of obesity. She had lost one hundred and twenty-seven pounds. In the seven years since, she hadn't regained more than five. Swimming laps for an hour every day was a big part of her weight-loss program, along with taking three-mile walks three times a week. She was immensely proud of the fact she had taught herself to enjoy foods that were body friendly.

Hearing the sound of a piano from the house next door, Octavia stopped in the middle of changing her clothes to listen to the pleasant music.

I guess the new owners have moved in. I'll have to get them a welcome gift, she thought.

She finished changing her clothes, grabbed a bath sheet, and went out to her pool.

When she finished her swim an hour later, the music was still playing. It was so pleasant and tranquil that she stretched out on a lounge chair to enjoy it.

Closing her eyes, Octavia thought back over the years. She thought about how she had overcome the crippling unhappiness she'd experienced in high school when she was teased and harassed unmercifully about her weight. She thought about how she longed to be thin and beautiful like the other girls at school. She thought about the names she was called.

The name she hated most was "Octavia Octagon." The kids would call her this, saying, "Because she has so many sides, you have to stop when you look at her."

Octavia hadn't had any friends. She felt she couldn't trust anyone's friendship. Anytime anyone had befriended her, it always ended with that person playing a cruel trick on her. She remembered the deep hurt that made her cry herself to sleep every night.

Then Octavia thought of Professor Bradford Harrington, her college English professor, and smiled. The professor had pulled her aside after class one day during her freshman year and asked if she had ever considered writing as a career.

"You have such flair to your writing that I believe you could be a great novelist," he said.

Professor Harrington and his wife, Dora, became Octavia's mentors. They invited her to book readings, first on campus, then at book stores, and later at their home.

Octavia was so happy to have honest interactions with others that she became comfortable sharing her thoughts and feelings for the first time in her life. She told Professor and Mrs. Harrington how it felt to be a foster child, and how unsettling it was to not have any family to call her own.

Octavia shared the heartbreaking event that had occurred when she was with her last foster parents, the Franklins. On her eighteenth birthday, she hadn't even received a birthday card. On that same day, the social worker had shown up at 6:00 a.m. and informed her that she had to vacate the home immediately because another child was coming in. Octavia was transported to a transition house and told she had two weeks to find herself an apartment and get a job. She was not a minor anymore, they told her, and the state would no longer support her.

She told the Harringtons about the counselor at the transition house who seemed like a guardian angel and helped her get a scholarship to the state college.

"If it hadn't been for her," Octavia cried, "I don't know what would have happened to me. I know that she was just doing her job, but when she dropped me off at my studio apartment near the campus, hugged me and wished me good luck, it was the first time in my life that I could remember anyone hugging me."

The Harringtons were compassionate people who freely showed their love to one another, and they also expressed love for Octavia. They began treating her like a daughter, visiting her at her apartment when she didn't check in with them daily.

They showered her with advice, compliments, attention, and gifts. It didn't take long for Octavia to consider them as her parents. They were so kindhearted that she began calling them Mom and Pop Harrington, much to their joy and delight.

It was Mom Harrington who suggested Octavia start to exercise and experiment with body-friendly foods.

During the summer between Octavia's freshman and sophomore year, Mom Harrington had to have double-knee surgery. "Octavia, dear," she said, "I need someone to come to the gym with me and help me through my rehabilitation. Would you help me? Brad and I are more than willing to pay you for your time. It can be your summer job."

Octavia didn't think twice about the invitation. "I'd be more than happy to help you," she said. "Thank you for asking."

As a result of that situation, Octavia showed up on campus to start her second year of college fifty pounds lighter and one hundred percent happier. She enjoyed being with Mom Harrington and treasured the time spent helping her, but she mostly enjoyed the feeling she got when she used the machines and felt her muscles develop. Soon her body began to change shape.

For the remainder of her college career, Octavia stayed close to the kind and loving couple. They encouraged her in her school work just as they encouraged her in her efforts to lose weight. They were with her when she lost the last twenty pounds and had surgery to remove the unwanted skin.

Mom and Pop Harrington were in the audience when Octavia received the Writers Guild Award for her first book, *A Journey to Myself.* They were so proud of her that when she went to their home after the ceremony, she found that they'd planned a surprise party. It was the first party she had ever had in her life.

Feeling the change in temperature and looking up to the darkening sky, Octavia said aloud, "Lord, I'm so grateful for those two angels in my life. Thank you."

With that, she grabbed her towel and went inside to take a shower and put on her housecoat and slippers.

CHAPTER 2
Welcome to the Neighborhood

It became a nightly ritual for Octavia to come home, swim a few laps, and spend the rest of the evening doing chores or writing a few ideas on paper while listening to the beautiful piano music from her next-door neighbors. She still had not met them, but she was determined that this weekend she would get them a gift and introduce herself.

That resolution, however, was a little hard to keep. On Friday night, Octavia had a book reading for her latest novel. Saturday was Mom and Pop Harrington's forty-fifth wedding anniversary, and she was having a surprise party for them at her house. On Sunday, she planned to climb back into bed after church and read the newspaper from the first to last page.

"Oh well," she said to herself, "I'll figure something out."

Thursday afternoon before leaving work, Octavia checked with the caterer, the party planner, and finally, the florist.

While she was on the phone with the florist, she asked him, "Do you have anything that says welcome to the neighborhood?"

The florist assured her that a picturesque planter full of beautiful wildflowers would be delivered to her neighbors by noon the next day. Feeling satisfied, Octavia worked to clear her desk and shut down her office. She went home feeling like she had accomplished her goals for the day.

Turning onto her street, Octavia saw a car in the new neighbor's driveway and noticed no music coming from the home.

Oh, she thought, *they have company. I'm going to miss the music tonight.*

It was just as well. She had a lot to do to get ready for the Harringtons' anniversary party, and she really didn't need the music to distract her.

By the time she had taken care of all her chores and laid the groundwork for the party planners to arrive early on Saturday morning, Octavia was tired.

It's a good thing I don't have any classes tomorrow, she thought. *I'm going to sleep late and go shopping for the anniversary gift before the book reading and signing reception at the Mid-town Book Emporium.*

She locked up for the night, and just as she turned off the lights and lay in her bed, the music began. But tonight, it was not soft and melodious. It was severe and discordant.

Wow, wonder what they are angry about? she thought as she drifted off to sleep.

Octavia kept her promise to herself to sleep late, so it was almost ten o'clock when she left her house to go shopping. As she opened her front door to get her mail and pick up the newspaper, she saw a note had been placed under her welcome mat to keep it from blowing away. She picked it up and opened it. There were two words written in calligraphy on the paper: *Thank you!* It was signed *Sebastian.*

Well, she thought, *I guess that's the new neighbor, and the planter must have been delivered.*

She put the note in her purse, closed her door, and went shopping. It was after six o'clock when she returned from the day's activities. She looked at her neighbor's yard and there was the planter, sitting near the footpath at the end of the front door landing. It looked beautiful.

CHAPTER 3
Get the Party Started

Getting Mom and Pop Harrington to the surprise party was a lot easier than Octavia thought it would be. She decided to be straightforward. "Pop, can you and Mom come over tonight for an anniversary dinner?" she asked.

"Of course," he replied, "we'd love to come to your beautiful home. What time?"

Since the happy couple would be there by 6:15, the guests were told to arrive no later than 5:55. The last thing that had to be done was to write a note to the new neighbors, the Sebastians, to let them know she was having a patio party and that it would last until midnight at the latest. She apologized in advance for any inconvenience.

Octavia dashed across the lawn, but before she could leave the note or ring the bell, the door was snatched open. She looked up into a face that seemed vaguely familiar, even through the scowl that was on it now.

"What?" the man growled.

"Good after—" Octavia began, then continued, "I was going to leave this note for you. I wasn't sure if you were home or not."

She handed the man the note and quickly ran back to her house. When she got to her porch, she looked across the lawn to get another look at the familiar stranger, but he had quickly stepped back into his house and slammed the door.

"Surprise! Happy Anniversary!" everyone shouted when the Harringtons stepped out of the house into Octavia's beautifully decorated backyard.

"Young one, what have you done?" Mom Harrington said. "This is wonderful."

The party was a success. Everyone had a good time, and the guests of honor were pleased with the state of affairs. Everyone seemed to get along well. The attendees seemed to find their own groups, and the conversations flowed freely.

Octavia went to the kitchen to get more punch. Earlier, she had combined pineapple juice, sliced lemons, and orange juice in large containers and was just adding champagne to another batch when someone stepped through the door.

Not paying attention, she pointed to the hall on the other side of the kitchen. "The bathroom is just through the door down the hall on the right," she said without looking up from the punch bowl.

"I'll keep that in mind in case I'm looking for it later," a smooth, pleasant voice replied. Octavia looked up into the handsome face of Professor Matthew Scott Edwards. He smiled and said, "I just came to see if you needed help carrying the punch bowl, Professor Peterson."

"I'll let you do just that if you promise to call me Octavia," she said, stepping back from the punch bowl. "Thank you. It is heavy when it's full. You take this out, and I'll bring out some more salads and another meat platter."

For the rest of the night, it seemed that Professor Edwards was right there to offer a helping hand whenever she needed assistance. After the party, he didn't leave until all of the tables and chairs had been folded and piled in the shed so they could be picked up on Monday morning.

"This was a great party, Octavia," he said. "I'm glad I came."

Professor Matthew Edwards was a very handsome man. He was

extremely well-groomed and very poised; he seemed to radiate confidence and self-assurance. His voice was so smooth that it was almost hypnotic. To Octavia, the man was *fine!*

"Thank you for coming, Professor," Octavia said, smiling broadly, breathing softly.

When she reached out to shake his hand, he took it and pulled her in to a quick and unexpected hug. "As you know," he whispered into her ear, "I'm new in town, and I need a tour guide. Would you be my guide, Octavia?"

When they broke the embrace, she looked into his eyes and uttered one word, "Yes," breathlessly.

CHAPTER 4
First Date

After giving the professor her information and saying the final good-nights, Octavia gave her house and back yard a final inspection. Later, as she was stepping out of the shower, she heard a familiar sound. Her neighbor, Mr. Sebastian, was playing that haunting melody again.

It's two o'clock in the morning, she thought. *I wonder if they ever sleep over there.* She yawned, climbed into bed, and as usual the music was so soothing that Octavia went to sleep with a satisfied smile on her face.

Intending to keep her promise to herself, Octavia headed straight home after church the next morning. She turned on the tea kettle and changed her clothes while the water was heating. By the time she had on her silk pajamas, the kettle was whistling, and she made a large mug of strawberry green tea.

Before she was able to get into her bed, the phone rang. It was Professor Edwards.

"You're finally home," he said. "How was church this morning?"

"Good afternoon, Professor Edwards," Octavia said, "church was wonderful. The sermon was about living life God's way."

"That sounds good. Maybe I can go with you one Sunday."

"I would like that, Professor, and I'm sure you would enjoy yourself, too."

"Thank you, it's a date. But while that's a ways off, would you have dinner with me tonight?"

Octavia was excited when she hung up the phone. She ran to her closet and spent the next hour trying to find the right outfit to wear to the first date she'd ever had.

By the time 5:30 in the evening came around, she was dressed in a black two-piece dress with red shoes and a matching clutch purse. Her hair was combed in a simple, no-bangs pageboy, and she had on gold hoop earrings with a matching gold single-strand wheat chain necklace, bracelet, and watch.

When the doorbell rang, Octavia almost jumped out of her chair. She slowly walked to the front door. "Good evening, Professor Edwards," she said.

He smiled and stepped through the door to help her with her wrap. "It would be a better evening if you were to call me Matthew instead of Professor Edwards," he said with a dazzling smile.

Dinner was perfect, as was the whole date. Matthew Edwards was a perfect gentleman; Octavia didn't have to try hard to impress her date. He'd had everything pre-planned. When they arrived at the restaurant, they were seated immediately, and the wine was served. When the menus were offered, Matthew said, "Don't worry about ordering, Octavia. If you don't mind, I selected our meals when the reservation was made."

His bright smile made everything seem even more perfect, so she relaxed and allowed the date to unfold as he had planned.

After dinner, they strolled along the waterfront causeway, engaged in casual conversation, stopping occasionally to watch the flocks of geese coming and going. When they arrived back at Octavia's house, Matthew escorted her to the front door, thanked her for a comfortable evening, gave her a quick hug, and did not pull out of the driveway until she was inside.

As she showered and dressed for bed, Octavia thought about how pleasant the date had been.

I don't have anything to compare it to, but I'd say that my first date was a true success, she thought as she sat at the vanity brushing her hair and smiling until her face hurt.

CHAPTER 5
First Love

It wasn't long before the two professors became an item. They managed to have lunch together twice a week and had dinner together every Wednesday after prayer service. Three weekends in succession, they traveled to tourist sites in the area. It seemed they were a compatible, well-matched couple.

Matthew Edwards was all man. He had a dynamic, compelling, and authoritative personality that worked well for him. Octavia enjoyed how he handled situations. He never seemed to waver when there was a problem to be solved.

He was even supportive of Octavia's efforts to maintain a healthy lifestyle. He reserved the campus workout room two days a week and worked out with her, offering tips about which machines and exercises would benefit her most.

"You know," he told her during one workout session, "you would benefit from a meatless diet two days a week. You would have better muscle tone, especially in your upper arms and thighs, if you didn't eat so much protein."

Because she had begun to trust him, Octavia took his suggestion and saw results within a month.

One evening when the happy couple was sitting on the patio after dinner, Octavia's neighbor began playing.

"Oh, this is so wonderful," she said. "I love these evening piano concerts."

But Matthew was not so pleased with the musical offering. "That's ridiculous. How often does that happen? I'm going over there and demand they have some respect for their neighbors!"

Just as Matthew was getting out of his seat, Octavia touched his arm. "Please don't do that. I enjoy listening to the music. It's so soothing to me."

"Well, *I* don't like it, and *I* don't have to listen to it if *I* don't want to," he said. "And I'm not having it."

Matthew stood and crossed the yard. By the time Octavia caught up with him, he was trying to unlatch the gate that led to the neighbors' back yard. "Matthew, stop, don't do this, please."

He turned and looked at her with burning eyes. "Well, you do something about it, or I'm leaving."

Octavia stepped back and looked at him, shocked. "I'm not going to cause any trouble with my neighbor because of a little piano playing, Matthew. Let's just sit back down and enjoy it."

"You sit back down and enjoy it," he said, then turned away from her, stormed back to the patio table, snatched his keys, and left the yard through the corridor between the house and the garage. "Good night, Octavia, enjoy your concert."

The next afternoon, Octavia left the Humanities building after her last class and caught a glimpse of Matthew. She wasn't sure if she should try to get his attention or not. Just then, he turned and looked at her but didn't speak. He didn't even return her wave.

For the next two weeks, Octavia didn't see or hear from Matthew. Then on Wednesday, while she was at prayer service, someone sat next to her. "I don't seem to have my Bible with me. Do you mind if we share?"

Matthew was smiling at her with twinkling eyes. Octavia smiled at him in return and slid her Bible over for him to share.

"I'm so sorry about what happened. I hope you can forgive me. I acted like a real jerk," was his explanation as they stood by her car after the service. "Have dinner with me? We need to talk."

Octavia shook her head. "I'm going to go straight home tonight. Let's talk some other time. I'm tired."

Taking hold of her arm, Matthew replied, "Come on, Octavia, you don't have anything else to do. It won't take long. We can have a quick salad."

She couldn't resist. "Oh, okay, Matthew, a quick salad."

The "quick salad" took two hours. As Matthew was walking her to her front door, the sound of the neighbor playing the piano was resonating melodiously across the yard.

"I still don't like that invasion," Matthew said, "but I guess I have to accept it if you and I are going to be together." He gave Octavia a hug and a quick kiss on the cheek. "Good night," he said as got in his car and left.

CHAPTER 6
Summer Break

The spring semester was coming to a close, and Octavia was excited about the coming summer activities. She had signed up for two cruises. The first was the Puget Sound cruise, a three-week land and water tour Mom and Pop Harrington had asked her to join them on. The second was a Caribbean cruise, again with Mom and Pop Harrington. Between the cruises, Octavia had plans to spend two weeks on the East Coast taking the Underground Railroad tour, which began in Maryland and ended in Ontario, Canada.

"So what am I supposed to do while you are away? How can you desert me like this?" Matthew asked her.

"You'll be teaching your classes," she replied. "Besides, I had these trips planned before you and I even knew one another." She gave him a sad smile. "Don't try to make me feel guilty. It won't be so bad. We'll see each other when I come home to change suitcases."

Traveling was a new experience for Octavia. This was her first cruise. She and the Harringtons arrived in Port Townsend a day early to ensure they correctly followed all instructions from the cruise line directive. After reporting to the cruise line check-in station, Octavia was assigned her cabin and given an official cruise itinerary. Then she, Mom, and Pop went to the nearest hotel and checked in.

She asked the hotel desk clerk for information on the evening's entertainment.

"The Seattle Symphony Orchestra is presenting their first summer concert tonight, and they are featuring a guest musician," the clerk told her.

The Harrisons were tired from the trip and decided to spend a quiet night in their hotel room before the cruise, so Octavia made arrangements for the hotel shuttle to take her to the concert.

It was held at the Water's Edge Amphitheater, and Octavia had a great seat—she could see the entire stage from the center of the tenth row. The concert was titled Summer Breeze. Octavia was so excited that she could hardly sit still as she waited for the show to begin.

Finally, the lights dimmed. In the dark, a lone figure walked to the grand piano and began playing a haunting melody. It was a melody familiar to Octavia. It sounded like the one her next-door neighbor always played.

The pianist's extraordinary talent was exhibited in his skillful manipulation of the keys. His opening performance was so stirring that he received a standing ovation.

As lights slowly illuminated the stage, the announcer spoke. "Ladies and gentlemen, please join the members of the Seattle Symphony Orchestra in welcoming our special guest, master musician extraordinaire, Sebastian. He will be presenting several more of his original arrangements tonight, and let me assure you, they're all just as magnificent as his opening piece."

Octavia looked at the tall, smiling, well-dressed man now standing beside the baby grand piano. She thought, *Oh, my goodness, that's him!* She smiled a secret smile and sat back to enjoy the concert.

So my new neighbor is Sebastian, the musical genius, she thought. *No wonder he looked so familiar.*

Suddenly, Octavia remembered him. Sebastian Warwick was a boy she'd gone to high school with. He had been nice to her, but back then he'd been a nerd with his own battles to fight. Knowing that she and the guest musician had a common bond made the concert more enjoyable for Octavia. She settled back in her seat and let the music engulf her.

Later in her hotel room, Octavia was too excited to sleep. With the vision of Sebastian in his white tuxedo playing his original compositions, she lay in bed and hummed a tune from the concert. Suddenly, the bedside phone rang, startling her.

"You sound awfully happy for this time of night," Matthew said. "Where have you been? I've called your cell phone at least a half-dozen times. Finally, I had to call Professor Harrington's cell number to find out what was going on."

"Oh, hello, Matthew," Octavia replied, "how are you this lovely evening? I'm fine, thank you."

Mathew sounded exasperated. "Where have you been?"

Octavia stopped smiling. "I went to a concert. Why are you in such an awful mood?"

"I'm not in an awful mood. I was just worried about you, that's all. I'm beginning to hate that I even let you go on this trip. You should be here with me. I miss you."

Let me go? Octavia thought. *I don't need his permission to travel.*

But instead of speaking her thoughts, she soothed his feelings and told him she would be home before he knew it. Then she said good night and set the phone back down on its cradle.

It took her another half hour to fall asleep. Matthew's comment about "letting her go" on this trip caused a slight mental discomfort.

"We will have to have a talk when this cruise is over," she said aloud.

CHAPTER 7
The Cruise of a Lifetime

When the trio boarded the cruise ship, they were greeted by the captain and his supervisory staff. After check-in, Octavia took the activities tour of the ship. She decided she was going to enjoy her time aboard this floating luxury hotel.

The first thing she did after unpacking was knock on the other bedroom door of the suite and ask the Harringtons if they wanted to go to lunch.

"I understand that the food on these ocean cruises is so good you can gain as much as ten pounds after only a week," she said as they entered the main dining room.

During lunch, Octavia had the Harringtons complete their activities cards and turn them in to the cruise director. She was determined that they would have almost as much fun on this trip as she was going to have.

Octavia's first onboard adventure was to learn how to mountain trek, and then she was going to surf. The mountain trek activities involved a three-day training session. The first two days' activities would begin at 8:00 a.m. and end at 11:30 a.m. The final day would begin at 6:45 a.m. and would include a simulated mountain climb.

"Oh, my goodness," Octavia said to Mom and Pop afterward, "I had such a great time. I might be ready to climb a real mountain after this." She was smiling broadly. "I'm so proud of myself. This is the first time I've stepped outside of my box and had an adventure like this. It was the most intense and passionate thing I've ever done."

Even though the last three days had been intense, with the body training sessions leaving her muscles feeling stretched tight but strong, completing the climb left Octavia feeling satisfied and competent.

"So is that sore, stiff body of yours going to be able to go to the Big Band Sound Ballroom dance with us tonight?" Mom Harrington asked.

Octavia laughingly said, "You bet I will. I don't want to miss my chance to see you two do that old-timers dancing I've heard about."

"Don't laugh at us, young lady," Mom Harrington warned. "You young people today don't know how to dance. What you do is gyrate to loud noise and strong beats. Back in our day, we listened to the music and communed with one another as we swayed to the soft, melodious compositions."

"Oh, really, Mom? Then what do you call the mambo, the samba, and the jitterbug?"

Mom Harrington tapped Octavia on the shoulder and said, "Just hush, you young thing."

Everyone had a good laugh.

Pop said, "We'll hopefully see you then, young lady, but for now, we're going to the seafood buffet."

They kissed her gently on the cheeks and joyfully walked out of their suite, leaving their beloved adopted daughter to her slight misery.

As tempting as the seafood buffet sounded, Octavia was enticed more by the idea of taking a nap, so she piled her pillows around her sore body and slept. Later, after a warm shower, she dressed in a midnight-blue cap sleeve dress with a feather patterned sequined V-neck front, a cinched sequined waistline, and a knee-length flared skirt. Then she slipped her feet into her satin shoes and fastened the straps around her ankles, picked up her matching purse, checked her hair that had been pinned into an elegant upsweep, and looked in the mirror.

She was surprised to see the outfit and style were very becoming of her. "Girl," she said to her reflection, "you need to marry someone who can dress you like this all the time. You look good!"

She laughed at herself, then glided out the door and to the ballroom.

"Well, Sleeping Beauty, it's good to see you. We didn't think you were going to make it," Mom Harrington said with a smile.

Octavia, returning the smile, looked at the elegant and very dignified-looking couple sitting at table number 27 on the edge of the ballroom dance floor. They looked so attractive: Pop Harrington, well-shaved with his neatly combed crop of salt-and-pepper hair, was dressed in a vintage 1940s-style black tuxedo with tails. His pants had a satin stripe down the legs, and the vest and bow tie were patterned in small black-and-gray check.

Mom Harrington looked equally as stunning. Her hair was coiffed elegantly in a French braid, intricately woven with thin strands of multi-colored sequin ribbons, and she was dressed in a chic mid-arm cap sleeve floor-length black rayon cocktail dress with a wrap front that tied at the waist. The dress was accented with a multi-colored bird of paradise appliqué that began with the bird's head on the left shoulder and crossed her body to end at her right hip.

Almost immediately, the band started playing "Moonlight Serenade." Without delay, the Harringtons were on the floor and stayed there for almost every selection the band played.

Octavia was happy to see the couple let down their guard and enjoy themselves. It didn't bother her that she was one of the few unescorted attendees. She was content to sit and watch her mentors having fun. After all, this cruise was about them.

After the band played three songs, someone came to her table and asked, "Professor Peterson, would you like to dance?"

Octavia looked up at a young man named Charles Kester, whom she had taught at least three years ago. He was in a ship officer's uniform.

"Well, yes, young man, I would like to dance, thank you," she said with a curious smile.

As they danced, Charles told her that his parents were half owners of the cruise line and he was learning the business from bow to stern. For this cruise, he was functioning as part of the entertainment staff.

"So," he said, "when I saw you sitting alone, Professor, I thought I would come over and have a dance with you."

By the end of the night, the two had become well acquainted. At one point, Charles shared his plans for the future and seemed genuinely pleased when Octavia encouraged him to follow his dreams. When the evening's activities were coming to a close, Charles asked for one last dance.

As Octavia and the Harringtons walked back to their cabin, Pop Harrington teased Octavia. "So we see you've made a friend! Does this mean there's going to be an onboard romance?"

Octavia stopped in mid-step. "Pop! Oh, my goodness . . . stop teasing me like that. He's a former student of mine who took pity on me because I was sitting alone at the table while you two were marathon dancing."

To change the subject, Mom Harrington asked, "What are your plans for tomorrow, young one? I could use an exercise partner. What time are you planning on getting up?"

The ladies agreed to 7 a.m. and said goodnight as they each entered their suites.

Before leaving for the dance, Octavia had left her cell phone in her room so she could enjoy the evening. Now, as she checked her email and text messages, she saw there were four . . . all from Matthew.

The first message was a quick greeting: *Sweetheart, just wanted to say hello.* The second message read, *Haven't heard from you in a couple of days, hope you're having fun.* The third was short and abrupt: *What are you doing?*

His final communiqué was a little intense: *Octavia . . . You need to contact me as soon as you get this message!*

She turned on her computer and sent a message that she would be on Skype by 10:00 a.m. Pacific Coast time tomorrow.

After combing her hair and changing into her pajamas, Octavia stepped onto the patio deck outside the suite's entertainment nook. It was a beautiful night with a clear blue sky and lots of twinkling stars. She stood breathing in the refreshing sea air until her eyes began to feel heavy and her body was relaxed and tranquil.

CHAPTER 8
Having Fun

When she returned from the workout session with Mom Harrington, Octavia took extra care with her grooming. She donned a cheerful sundress with a short-sleeved jacket; she put her hair back in the same style from the previous night and even put on makeup. She wanted to look good for Matthew.

Promptly at 10:00 a.m. Pacific Coast time, she signed in to Skype and Matthew was right there, looking as handsome as ever.

"It's about time I heard from you, Miss Peterson. I was thinking you were having so much fun that you'd forgotten me."

"Hello, Matthew," she said, smiling, "it sounds like you miss me. But don't worry, we have only two more weeks and the cruise will be over. Then we'll have a week to spend together. I'll be glad to see you."

For the next half hour, they made small talk. When the call ended and she closed her computer, Octavia caught a glimpse of someone standing in the shadow by the railing. When she gave the figure her full attention, the man stepped into the sunlight. It was Sebastian Warwick.

"Good morning, I hope I didn't scare you," he said, standing on the patio next door with his hands in his pockets. "I heard you talking and your voice sounded familiar, so I came out to see if it was really you. Howdy, neighbor." He grinned sheepishly. "Since we're neighbors even aboard this ship, I think we should have breakfast together and get acquainted." He looked at his watch. "Although at this time I should say brunch. What do you say? Would you have brunch with me?"

Octavia tried hard not to let her mouth hang open. "What are you doing here?" was all she could manage to say. She was surprised to see him this close.

As they were going through the buffet line, Sebastian noticed what Octavia was putting on her plate. When they sat down to eat, he asked with a secretive smile, "So, how much weight have you lost?"

She looked at him with her own enigmatic expression and said, "You first."

After they both laughed, he kindly said, "So, you do remember me."

"Of course I do, but it wasn't until the Summer Breeze concert last week that I put it all together."

"You were there?" he asked, surprised.

"Yes, and I enjoyed it immensely. You were mesmerizing in your white tuxedo, playing that shiny black grand piano with the spotlights on you."

"Why didn't you come backstage after the concert to say hello?" he asked.

Octavia looked down at her plate. "Oh, I couldn't have done that. I wasn't dressed to meet a star."

"Well, I saw you at the dance last night, and you looked beautiful."

Octavia mumbled a quick "thank you" as she picked at the food on her plate.

"And I didn't come over because you were being entertained by an officer," he continued with a smile. Then he reached across the table and touched her hand. "I'm not a star," he whispered, leaning forward.

They looked at each other for a few seconds, and he pulled his hand away as she released her fork and put her hand in her lap.

"Two hundred," Sebastian said. "I've lost two hundred pounds. I went to Julliard after graduation, and the studies were so intense that most of the time, I would forget to eat. So by the time I'd lost seventy-five pounds, I liked the way it felt and started working out and searching for a diet that worked with my new lifestyle. What about you?"

She offered a smile. "I started losing weight the summer between my freshman and sophomore years of college. By the time I finished undergrad, I'd lost ninety pounds. Altogether, I've lost one hundred twenty-seven pounds."

Sebastian nodded, then said, "I'd like to talk longer, but I have rehearsal. Would you be my guest tonight at the Midnight Serenade?"

He looked so hopeful that Octavia quickly said, "Yes."

Sebastian reached across the table, lifted her hand, and kissed it. As he was walking away, the Harringtons stopped at the table. "So, Dad, our little girl is growing up," Mom Harrington said, giving Octavia a fake scowl.

Pop Harrington chuckled. "Well, young lady, what do you have to say for yourself? We leave you alone for one hour, and here you are with another young man. And this one is kissing your hand. Scandalous!"

Octavia spent the rest of the day wondering why she agreed to go to the midnight concert. She wanted to tell Sebastian that she had changed her mind, but she didn't see him anywhere. He didn't show for the late lunch or dinner, and she didn't see him at the pool or on any of the decks as she was walking and meeting other passengers.

Finally, at seven o'clock, she decided to keep her commitment. She laid out the outfit and shoes she was going to wear. Then she laid herself down for a nap.

An hour and a half before the concert was to begin, Octavia was dressed and sitting in the entertainment room of her suite. "I don't know why I'm so nervous about going to hear some musicians playing and singing," she said to herself. "It's just a concert. What's wrong with me?"

A light tap on the door startled her. As she opened it, Sebastian stepped through and handed her a wrist corsage. "I was hoping you were ready. I want to take a walk before the concert begins. Will you take a walk with me, Octavia Peterson?" When she agreed, he added, "You should probably grab a light wrap. The late-night air is pretty breezy on the water."

After doing just that, Octavia took his gloved, outstretched hand, and they walked out of the cabin.

Just outside the cabin door, Sebastian offered his arm to Octavia. "I hope you don't mind my arm. I'm wearing these gloves because I'm warming my hands for tonight's performance."

Octavia added a little pressure to his arm and smiled. "It's alright, I understand."

They walked through the maze of corridors and up to the ship's top deck. Standing at the railing looking out over the calm Pacific waters, Sebastian spoke in an almost muted tone. "Tonight's presentation is the first in a series of concerts that we'll be presenting this season. I asked you to come so we could get some feedback from you. An evaluation, so to speak. Do you mind?"

Octavia shook her head. "I don't mind. In fact, I'm honored that you think I could be of some assistance to a distinguished musician like yourself."

CHAPTER 9
Oh, What a Night

The concert was being held on the upper entertainment deck, and tonight it was set up much like an amphitheater. Chairs were set up facing the vast picture windows so that the stage appeared to be floating among the stars. Sebastian escorted Octavia to the very back row of chairs.

"This is probably the best seat in the house," he said, "and if you sit here, I'll know where you are, and I can pretend we're playing just to you." Before leaving her, Sebastian handed Octavia a booklet. "This is our program for tonight, and it's for your eyes only."

While the musicians were busy tuning up and the singers warmed their vocal cords, and while the audience entered the hall, she reviewed the evening's agenda. The program featured a wide variety of classic and contemporary songs, both instrumental and vocal.

The concert, Midnight Serenade, was aptly named. From the moment the members of the jazz band orchestra took the stage, the audience was awed. A concert of love songs played expertly by the musicians and sung passionately by the vocalists reduced many audience members to tears.

Some in the audience sang along with the singers, swaying to the rhythmic offerings, and some even left their seats and danced on the small dance floor in front of the bandstand.

After the show, and after the last of the audience had exited the concert hall and the musicians had packed their instruments, Sebastian returned and sat down beside Octavia.

"So what did you think?" he asked.

"It was an amazing presentation," Octavia said. "I've never been so emotionally entangled with music before. This was more than a concert. It was like listening to a love story in poetry and music."

Without saying another word, Sebastian stood, wrapped a scarf around his neck, and after he pulled on a pair of gloves, he took Octavia by the elbow and helped her from her seat. Then he laid her wrap around her shoulders and they stepped out onto the deck, arm in arm.

Instead of going directly to Octavia's cabin, the couple walked around the deck and stood by the railing to watch the moonlight skim across the waves on the ocean.

"That day that you brought the note to my door," Sebastian said, "I recognized you right away, but I didn't think you recognized or even remembered me."

When Octavia did not reply, he continued. "I wanted to talk to you in high school, but I just couldn't seem to get the courage to step outside of myself and my situation and reach out to you."

"High school seems like a lifetime ago," Octavia said. "It's taken a while to recover from the childish pranks and cruel tricks that were inflicted on me, but I think I've managed to stop letting those things hinder me. It's been a long, hard journey, but I'm beginning to see the light at the end of the tunnel." There was a faint smile on her face and a faraway look in her eyes.

Sebastian smiled. "I never thought it mattered much to you. I thought you let it roll off your back, so to speak, like I did most of the time."

"Oh, it didn't roll off my back. I just held it in until I was alone. I would sometimes cry until I made myself sick. Then I turned to my best friend: food. It comforted me and made me feel good. It took my mind off the pain in my heart."

"It was my music that kept me occupied," Sebastian said. "I had some big shoes to fill. My parents were strict and unyielding. They had a vision for their children, and we had no say in it. As a result, everyone in my family has made a success of themselves. All except me, of course."

Octavia turned from the railing to face Sebastian. "I think that you are a fine musician, maybe the best I've ever heard. Why would you say such a thing about yourself?"

Sebastian smiled a distant smile and said, "My older brother owns his own business. He's the owner of a chain of men's fine apparel stores. My sister is a pediatric neurosurgeon. And then there's me, a piano player, the black sheep of the family." He gave a mirthless chuckle. "We had no time for socialization, and so I never had any friends . . . except music and food."

He looked at Octavia, his eyes sad and searching. "So as much as I hated to see what was happening to you, and as much as I wanted to offer you some comfort and support, I didn't have the emotional security to stand up for myself, much less anyone else."

In an attempt to avoid any more serious discussion about their past, they made small talk as they walked the deck. After about an hour, they made their way toward Octavia's cabin. When they arrived, Sebastian gently held Octavia by her shoulders and kissed her on each cheek and her forehead.

"Thank you," he whispered.

Once again, it was difficult for Octavia to go to sleep. Her mind was whirling. *Why did he kiss me like that?* she wondered. *And why did it feel so good?*

Her last thought before falling asleep was, *That wasn't enough. I wanted a real kiss.*

After two hours of sleep, Octavia awoke with a start. Her computer was sending an alarm that a message was being delivered. Jumping out of bed, she saw Matthew's picture flashing on her screen. She accepted his call and there he was on Skype, looking as self-assured and captivating as ever.

Octavia didn't get a chance to say much. "You look awful," Matthew said. "What have you been doing? I sure hope you're not trying to eat your way through the cruise. I've worked too hard trying to keep you on some type of diet for you to mess it up now."

For the next ten minutes, Octavia listened to Matthew tell her how hard he was working and how bored he was because she was on that silly cruise. And when it was time to say goodbye, Octavia could only wave and smile.

She was on her way to shower and dress for the docking when she saw an envelope on the floor by the cabin door.

Good Morning, Miss Octavia Peterson. Just a few lines to say thank you for last night and to say goodbye. I'm setting out this morning for San Francisco, then I'm on to Chicago, Boston, Philadelphia, and finally, New York. It's symphony season. (Smile) I hope to see you when this year's tour is over. Enjoy the rest of your cruise. S. W.

"Well, that's quite a surprise," she said to herself. "This morning is starting off with a strange twist. I hope things improve when we dock."

CHAPTER 10
Welcome Home

As the passengers left the ship, they were greeted by the Island Spa welcoming committee. Each member was guided to a specific person who would be their spa activities group director for the week.

The Island Spa Resort was situated on an islet that was small and uninhabited except for the owners and workers at the spa. It was rustic in style and modern in service. During the day, people participated in group activities like small-mountain climbing and cross-country trekking for the younger or more stalwart vacationers.

For others, the not-so-young and energetic, they offered services like seaweed wraps, mud baths, full-body moisture wraps, warm stone massages, sea salt scrubs, and full salon services, including manicures and pedicures.

All things considered, the spa week was captivating and enchanting. Octavia had a wonderful time enjoying the resort services, but always in the back of her mind was the evening she had spent with Sebastian Warwick and the pleasure that she felt when he kissed her in that most Victorian fashion.

By the end of the week, Octavia and the Harringtons were ready to return to their homes. "Vacations are nice, but going home afterward is even nicer," Pop Harrington said as they boarded the ship for a quick three-and-a-half-day sail back to Port Townsend, Washington.

For the three weary travelers, the trip home was an anxious experience. They had enjoyed their adventure but now wanted nothing more than to have a full night's sleep in their own beds.

Octavia dropped the Harringtons off at their house and went straight home. As soon as she pulled into the driveway and parked her car in the garage, Octavia felt the full force of fatigue come down on her.

Climbing out of the car, she didn't even bother to take her suitcase with her. She closed the garage door, used the disarming button on her keychain to turn off the house alarm, and stepped inside.

Standing in the alcove between her kitchen and the family room, looking around with a half-smile, she whispered to herself, "It's good to be home."

It was 1:45 a.m. Octavia wasted no time. She took a quick shower and immediately climbed into bed. She burrowed under her oversized summer comforter and fell into a deep sleep.

It was 11:00 a.m. when Octavia languidly rolled back her bed covers and fully stretched her arms and legs. Resisting the inclination to burrow back under the covers, she admonished herself.

"Come on, girl, you have to get up. You have things that need attending to before you leave next week."

Reluctantly, she got out of bed, retrieved her suitcase from the car, took another quick shower, dressed, and was back in her car exiting the garage by one o'clock.

She made several stops while she was out. First, she went to her office to check her class rosters for the upcoming semester. Next, she went to the post office to pick up and to extend the vacation hold on her mail. The last thing she did was go to the market to get some fresh fruits and vegetables.

Turning onto her street, Octavia saw a car in her driveway. It was Matthew! She could hardly contain her joy.

"Hello, I'm so glad to see you," Octavia said, a big smile on her face.

Matthew gave her a quick hug and stepped back. "Where have you been? I saw you at the post office and came straight over. I've been waiting here for thirty-five minutes. What took you so long to get there from here?"

With a slight frown, Octavia began to answer his questions. "Well, now, let me see," she said, "I started out at my office, then I went to the post office. Then I went to pay my utilities, and lastly, the market. Finally, I came home. And how are you?"

Without waiting for an answer, Octavia lifted her bags from her car, unlocked her front door, and left it open while she carried her groceries to the kitchen.

"You don't have to be such a smart aleck about it," Matthew said. "I just thought you would be here after I arrived and I got worried about you, that's all."

"That's so sweet of you, Matthew. Can you forgive me? I'm still getting used to having someone to care about me. What can I do to make it up to you?"

"Turn around and let me look at you. How much weight did you gain on that cruise? You look a little thicker than you did three weeks ago." He touched her arms, her back, and her hips.

She playfully slapped his hands. "You stop that," she said, smiling. "I've actually lost six pounds. What you're feeling is muscle. I participated in as many physical activities as I could while I was away." She reached out to hug him. "Now, you behave yourself."

Matthew accepted her hug. "That's good, because you know I can't be seen with a fatty. All my women have to be in shape." He smiled and kissed her deeply. "I have to go, but I'll be back in two hours. I want a steak and salad for dinner. Medium-well."

With that said, he walked out the front door, got in his car, and drove away.

CHAPTER 11
Big Misunderstanding

Unfortunately for Matthew, Octavia didn't have any food in the freezer, so there were no steaks for dinner. However, she had everything she needed for an exceptional tossed salad, and she had some chicken breasts that she had just purchased and some fresh fruit. This was what she had to offer Matthew when he came back.

"What is this? Where's the steak?" he asked.

"I don't have any steaks in the house," she said. "You do remember that I've been away for three weeks and I'm leaving again next week, don't you?" she added, looking at him quizzically.

"So? What does that have to do with you not having a steak to go with this salad? You certainly had enough time to go back to the store and get one. I don't want any chicken. I can get chicken any time. What have you been doing since I've been gone?"

Pushing herself away from the kitchen counter, Octavia walked to the back door. "Matthew," she said, "I'm really tired, and I think I want to be alone tonight. So please leave." She stood with one hand on the doorknob and one on her hip.

Matthew was mildly taken aback at her request. "What? How are you going to talk to me like that?" He walked over to Octavia and looked at her for several seconds. "You know I'm going to give you what you asked for. I'm going to leave now and give you some time to yourself. It's obvious you're not ready for company. Goodnight!"

He stopped in the door frame and turned back to look Octavia up and down.

"I don't believe for a minute that you gained muscle weight. You look flabby."

His words hurt her feelings, but Octavia excused them. *He's just upset about not getting his way. He was right. I could have gone to the store and gotten a couple of steaks while he was gone.*

Then she sat at the kitchen table and cried.

An hour after the incident with Matthew, Octavia was unpacking her suitcase, washing dirty clothes, and repacking for next week's trip. She was still upset but wasn't going to let his angry words destroy her joy and excitement.

When I get back from this trip, I think Matthew and I should have a talk. I think we need to set some boundaries in this relationship.

She finished packing and took a relaxing bubble bath. As she was dressing for bed, her telephone rang.

"I didn't know if you would be home by now or not. I hope this isn't a bad time to call."

She recognized the voice instantly. "Hello, Sebastian. Actually, no, this isn't a bad time at all. How are you?"

As he spoke, she could hear a smile in his voice. "I'm doing fine, thank you. You're probably wondering why I'm calling you, and to be truthful, I was just thinking about you and wanted to hear your voice. How was your week on Spa Island?"

Octavia smiled. "I'm wondering more about how you got my number. But I will tell you that the week at the resort was very pleasant. We had a delightful time."

She told him about some of the activities she participated in and the spa services that she took advantage of. After twenty minutes of small talk, Sebastian told Octavia he would be back home in four weeks and asked if she would have dinner with him at his house. With that date set, they wished one another a good night and ended their conversation.

Later that evening, as she was lying in bed, instead of dwelling on the disagreement she'd had with Matthew, Octavia found herself smiling and picturing her next-door neighbor sitting at a polished grand piano playing with his eyes closed and his head turned slightly to the left, looking very appealing in his white tuxedo.

That was the soothing image that finally helped her settle her nerves and fall into a deep and peaceful sleep.

CHAPTER 12
Situations

The next morning, Octavia was checking her travel itinerary when her doorbell chimed. Opening the door, she was asked to sign for a delivery of flowers and chocolate.

The card read *What happened between us was silly. Let's apologize and move on.*

She couldn't believe her eyes. What was Matthew talking about? Was he offering an olive branch?

Well, Octavia thought, *this will have to wait until I get back from the Underground Railroad tour.*

She had to visit the Harringtons before she left, so she gathered the flowers and the chocolate and drove to their townhouse on University Circle. Mom and Pop were overjoyed to see her, especially since she was bearing gifts. Several times during the visit, Octavia's cell phone rang or beeped, but she ignored it. She wasn't in the mood to deal with Matthew and his attitude, so she ignored his attempts to contact her and enjoyed her visit.

Matthew was used to having things his way, so when Octavia didn't answer her phone or respond to his text messages, he drove to her home, sat in the driveway, and waited for her to arrive.

Turning onto her street later that night, Octavia saw Mathew's car in her driveway. "Oh, what does he want?" she whispered. "I don't want to deal with him tonight."

Taking a deep breath, she drove into the driveway just as Matthew jumped from his car. "Where have you been?" he asked. "I've been calling you all evening. Why didn't you answer the phone or at least respond to my text messages?"

"Good evening, Matthew," she said. "I was visiting, and it's rude to talk on the phone when you're visiting someone."

Matthew stepped close to Octavia. "I know I'm getting too personal so early in our relationship, but I care about you, and I worry when I can't get in touch with you. Besides, I wanted to know if you accepted my apology. I was out of line the other day. Do you forgive me?"

There was that adorable look again and that compassionate tone in his voice. It was hard for Octavia to be mean to him. She smiled and touched his arm. "Matthew, I can forgive you if you promise it won't happen again."

Matthew looked at Octavia and folded her in an embrace. He kissed her passionately. "I know that you are a grown woman. And I know that you can probably handle yourself in most situations, but I care for you, and because I do, I can't help worrying about you when I don't know where you are."

After another rousing kiss, Matthew released Octavia from his encirclement. "Go into that house, young lady. And don't forget to dream about me."

He sat in his car until she drove into her garage and closed the door.

The night before her departure, Octavia took another long, soothing bubble bath. Just as she was stepping out of the tub, her bedside phone rang. When she answered it, her neighbor's serene and comforting voice floated across the line.

"Hello, Octavia, I had an amazing performance last night after I spoke with you, so I thought I would call you again tonight just to see if it happens again. I think you're my good-luck charm." Sebastian chuckled then asked, "You don't mind, do you?"

Octavia couldn't help smiling. "Of course I don't mind. Congratulations on the concert, but I don't think talking to me had anything to do with your success. It's your skill and passion that brings you success."

"Listen, woman," he said, "let me have my fantasy, please."

They both chuckled. Octavia asked Sebastian about the tour. She reminded him that she would be gone for the next two weeks, and he reminded her that they had a dinner date coming up. After more small talk, they said good night and hung up.

CHAPTER 13
The Thrill is Gone

Pop Harrington drove Octavia to the airport, then after her luggage was checked, he hugged her and said, "Have a good trip, little girl, and when you come back, we have a few things to talk about."

Octavia looked at Pop Harrington and leaned into his hug. "Poppa, is something wrong? Are you okay? Is something wrong with Mom?"

"No, child, nothing like that," he said with a smile. "We are just concerned about your relationship with Professor Edwards. We know this is new for you, and we want to have that talk with you that all good parents should have with their children."

Octavia's vision blurred as she tightened her hold on her adopted father. "Pop, I just love you two wonderful people. See you in a couple of weeks, and then we can have that talk, I promise."

Pop Harrington smiled and waved until Octavia had gotten through security, then he let that false smile fade. He loved Octavia like a daughter and didn't want to see her get hurt by anyone, much less someone like Matthew Edwards.

During the flight, Octavia had lots to think about. On the one hand, there was Matthew, so debonair and smooth that it was hard to resist him. He did, however, have a dark side that she didn't care for. He was selfish, conceited, controlling, and manipulative.

On the other hand, there was Sebastian Warwick, the class nerd who grew up to be a talented, creative, sensitive, and insightful man—not to mention that he was absolutely the most charming and endearing man she had ever met.

Octavia was pleased that he was showing interest in her, and to this point she hadn't had to step outside of herself to be with him. Sebastian was a giver, not a taker.

Two men in her life was a real surprise for Octavia. To this point, she'd had only one real date, and that was with Matthew, but she remembered the "almost" date she'd had years before with a boy whose name she couldn't—or didn't care to—remember.

He had gotten permission from her foster parents to take her out. He'd arrived in a timely manner and very politely addressed them. He had picked her up under the pretense of taking her to the movies but instead took her to the park, spread out a blanket, and tried to have sex with her while other boys were hiding in the bushes. By that Monday morning, the entire school had heard about the farce. It was an incident that only added more fuel to the teasing and shaming.

It was a humiliating experience she never wanted to experience again, so she turned away from the world and to her best friend, food. A friend that was always there and gave immediate pleasure, happiness, and contentment. Now that she thought back on it, she realized all the humiliation, shaming, teasing, and negativity had been the catalyst to her decision to write stories about joy and happiness.

Now she was a grown woman with a grown woman's desires. She wanted to share her life with someone other than her adoptive parents, her colleagues, or her writing. She wanted to experience love and companionship. Even though she never considered herself lonely, she was tired of being alone.

Octavia spent the first half of her flight trying to weigh the pros and cons of having the attention of two men in her life.

Finally, she thought to herself, *Why am I trying to decide who to go out with? I don't have to choose one over the other. I can consider both as suitors.*

CHAPTER 14
Someone Like Matthew Edwards

It was as a young man in high school when Matty realized he had a power most other boys didn't. Almost by accident, he discovered that his looks, his talents, and the manners his grandmother had taught him could, if used properly, get him certain privileges the other guys were not afforded.

Girls whose families were from the "right side of the tracks" didn't mind having him around. Once, he turned his attentions on a girl and was invited to have dinner with her family. The mother always smiled and acted politely, while the father always wanted to talk to him man-to-man, many times offering Matty a job that would help him "get a step up" in life.

All Matthew had to do was use his impeccable manners, his handsome smile, and pretend to be interested in their fat, ugly, shy, desperate, or senseless daughter and he would receive benefits above and beyond his wildest unsophisticated dreams.

He did get teased by the guys, but he didn't care. He was getting remunerations that benefited him in achieving his goals. So he let them talk and tease while he was getting the jobs that put money in his pocket and helped him build a decent bank account.

By the time he was ready to graduate from high school, Matthew had polished his skills to the point that he had become a charming, charismatic personality. He even won a full-ride athletic scholarship that he rolled over into a full-ride academic scholarship for his post-graduate work.

By the time Matthew Edwards was receiving his Ph.D. in educational counseling, he was also ready to marry, so he set his sights on the insecure, unenlightened daughter of a highly successful businessman.

It was a good situation for both. She was grateful to be married to a well-educated, sophisticated, polished, and confident man. He benefited from the monthly living expenses that his father-in-law insisted on giving them because "education is an honorable profession, but it makes paupers of its practitioners."

Matthew's father-in-law wanted to help his daughter and son-in-law be able to afford some of the extra pleasures in life for their children. Of course Matthew made a small attempt to protest, but in the end he accepted it on behalf of his wife and their future children.

Right now, for Matthew Edwards, this was the perfect time for Octavia to be gone. He would have the freedom to move his family into town. And since Octavia was independent and had her own home in an area outside of the university community, she would probably not meet his wife until he was ready to have them meet—after he was finished with Octavia and wanted to get rid of her.

A relationship with Octavia Peterson had great possibility in Matthew's eyes. She was a desperate, lonely woman who was easily manipulated. This could be a long run for him. She was virgin territory, as far as he was concerned. For all he knew, she had never had a real relationship and was ripe for the picking.

Matthew had already put Octavia through several tests, and she'd passed with flying colors. Oh, she had given a little resistance, but that was short-lived. All he had to do was pretend to be remorseful or send her flowers and candy, and she would give in and let him have his way.

Why? Because she wanted him to be her lover. If not him, it would be someone else anyway, so why shouldn't he be the one?

Matthew's plan was to accommodate Octavia as long as she compensated him for the privilege of being with him.

CHAPTER 15
The Men in Her Life

When Octavia returned from the Underground Railroad tour, she was worn. It was an experience she would never forget. Being immersed in the history of her ancestors for just a two-week period was enlightening, informative, and insightful. She felt stronger mentally, emotionally, and spiritually after having experienced the trials and tribulations of the American slaves and their desire to be free even at the risk of being killed.

She was no longer confused about the men in her life, and she seemed to understand that there was nothing wrong with affording herself the best. She was secure in the fact that she would no longer accept second-class citizenship treatment. From now on, it was top of the line or nothing at all.

Too many people struggled for too long so that I could be where I am today, and I won't let anyone consider me less than first-rate anymore, Octavia promised herself.

After stepping off the plane and walking through the terminal to the baggage claim area, Octavia was surprised to see Matthew. He was smiling, holding a single rose, and flashing the biggest, most welcoming smile she had ever seen.

"Welcome home, wandering stranger," he said, offering her the rosebud and giving her a hug.

The ride to Octavia's house was pleasant. Matthew asked about the tour and listened while she excitedly shared some of the main points of her experiences. When they arrived and stepped through her front door, several people shouted, "Welcome home!"

The surprise party lasted three hours. By the end, Octavia was too tired to do anything except take a shower and fall into bed.

The next morning, she woke at 9:30 and fixed a mug of tea. She intended to climb back into bed with it, but the doorbell rang. When she opened it, there was a very large houseplant sitting on her porch. The delivery person requested her signature and asked, "Where do you want this, Miss Peterson?"

Octavia directed him to put it by the side window just inside the front door. When he was gone, she read the card aloud: "To my good-luck charm. Welcome home. Regards, S.W."

She couldn't help smiling. The plant looked good in her entryway, like it belonged there, and she was thrilled Sebastian had remembered her homecoming date. Octavia was so pleased that she sat in the living room drinking her tea and looking at the beautiful, lush, dark-green foliage.

After about a half hour, the doorbell chimed again. When she opened the door, there stood Mom and Pop Harrington. Once the hugs and kisses were out of the way, Mom Harrington was the first to speak.

"Are you alone?" she asked.

Octavia nodded, and the two elders led her back into her living room. For the next hour, they had a serious parent-to-child conversation.

Pop Harrington got up from the easy chair he was sitting in, walked over to the sofa, and offered his gentle words to the crying young woman. "We're only telling you because we love you and don't want you to experience any public humiliation or embarrassment because you didn't know."

Mom Harrington stood and walked over to Octavia. She offered a sad smile and added, "I never liked him, from the first time I laid eyes on him. He's so smug and arrogant. He's acted like he owned you from the very beginning. And when Brad told me he was married, I immediately thought it would be news to you also. He's so self-righteous he probably thinks he has the right to treat women like they're his play toys. So you see, sweetheart, that's why we wanted to tell you personally before he gets you caught up in a scandal of some sort."

The Harringtons stayed with Octavia for the rest of the morning and afternoon. As they left, they hugged her reassuringly and suggested she take a nap to settle her nerves.

CHAPTER 16
Tonight is the Night

By early evening Octavia had rested, unpacked, washed her clothes, and was ready to go outside for a swim. That was where Matthew found her, on the patio, still damp from the refreshing dip in the pool. As he walked into the yard, he stood watching her for a few minutes, then put on his most charming smile and said, "Well, sleeping beauty, I'm glad to see you out and about, even if it is in your own back yard."

"Hello, Matthew," Octavia said, "how was your day today?"

Ten minutes later, Octavia found herself still listening to Matthew complain about his day, thinking, *I'll probably never ask him about his day again. Has he always been such a windbag?*

When he saw a slight smile cross Octavia's face, Matthew thought he was amusing her. He had no idea she had amused herself by calling him a windbag.

"Look at you," he said cheerfully, "being a good listener, and I'm just going on and on." He stood and took her by her hands to help her from the patio lounger. "Let's go in and I'll help you take a shower," he said with a smile, "then I can give you a proper welcome home. Girl, I've been wanting to get familiar with you in an up-close and personal way for months, but you were busy running all over this country, so tonight is the night."

Octavia broke his embrace and stepped back. She smiled warmly at him and said, "Why don't you go home and take a shower and get familiar with your wife?"

"Oh, so you know about my wife," Matthew replied. "So what? My marriage has nothing to do with what you and I have."

"Matthew," Octavia said, "you and I have nothing. I have no intention of letting you continue to deceive your wife by having a relationship with you. Please leave my property and do not come back here again."

"Who do you think you're talking to? This relationship is not over until I say it's over," Matthew countered. "Now I came here to have sex with you, and that's exactly what's going to happen. I haven't put this much time into you to get nothing in return. You owe me for my investment, so to speak, and now it's time to pay up."

Octavia snatched her arm away from Matthew's grasp. "I asked you to get off of my property! Good night!" she snapped, then turned to walk toward her patio doors.

Matthew quickly stepped between Octavia and the doors. "You really think you're in control of this situation, don't you? Well, you're wrong! I came here for one thing tonight, and I'm not leaving until I get it. We can do this in a civilized way, or I can take what I want. It's up to you, and you have ten seconds to make your decision."

CHAPTER 17
Knight in Shining Armor

I t was Thursday night, and Sebastian had just played the final chords to "Beauty," his favorite composition. He stood and walked to the side of the shiny black piano to show his appreciation for the audience's prolonged applause. As he was smiling and taking his final bow, he thought about his good-luck charm.

She should be home by now, and I would love to surprise her at the pool when she comes out for her evening swim.

Sebastian had a ten-day break before his next concert. The stage in the New York University concert hall needed emergency repairs, so the final concerts of the tour had been rescheduled. It had been a grueling tour, and he was glad for the unexpected but much-appreciated break.

Never before had Sebastian been so glad to get home. He'd had Octavia on his mind for most of the last three weeks. Something about her made him happy, and it scared him a little.

Friday afternoon, as the airport limousine delivered him to his house, Sebastian noticed a car in Octavia's driveway. *Looks like she has company,* he thought. *I'll just go in and relax, then watch for her to come out for her swim.*

Sebastian knew that it was ridiculous to think he could prepare dinner for Octavia tonight, so he decided he would ask her if she'd go to a restaurant with him. Then one day next week, he would prepare the feast of a lifetime he had promised her.

Just before sundown, Sebastian heard the gentle, steady, rhythmic splashing from next door. He knew he had about an hour before Octavia was finished with her swim, so he freshened up, selected a wine-colored two-piece relaxed-fit linen walking suit, and put on a pair of matching leather sandals.

Walking out of his back door, he heard a strong male voice coming from Octavia's yard. As he stopped to listen, Sebastian didn't like what he was hearing.

"I came here for one thing tonight, and I'm not leaving until I get it," was the first thing he heard the male voice say. The next thing he heard was, "We can do this in a civilized way, or I can take what I want. It's up to you, and you have ten seconds to make your decision."

Then he heard Octavia respond. "What I want is for you to leave my property now, or I'll call the authorities. I know you don't want that, Matthew."

At that, Sebastian unlatched the gate and stepped into Octavia's yard. "Is there a problem here?"

Matthew dropped Octavia's arm and turned toward the man who had just entered the yard. "This is none of your business, so go away. This is between me and my girlfriend."

"I am not your girlfriend," Octavia said. "Get out."

Looking directly at Matthew, Sebastian said, "I know you heard the lady's request. Be a gentleman and leave."

"And if I don't leave, what are you going to do about it, piano boy?"

Sebastian offered a disconcerting smile in answer to the question. Trying to push his advantage, Matthew sprang at Sebastian and immediately found himself face down on the ground.

Sebastian had merely sidestepped and, using the man's own momentum, pushed Matthew in his back. That sent Matthew flying out of control, and he landed on the ground on his face.

Jumping up, Matthew angrily charged again and was consequently flipped into the pool. After climbing out and standing soaking wet at the pool's edge, Matthew pointed at Sebastian. "This isn't over, piano boy. Next time we meet, it's personal between you and me." As he was walking away, he said over his shoulder, "You can have her. She's just a sad, pathetic, fat, desperate old maid anyway."

Octavia gasped. The words hurt her. She leaned down to retrieve her towel and wrapped it around her body. Then she turned to go into the house before the tears pooling in her eyes could fall, but Sebastian stepped into her path.

She pulled back, trying to escape the comforting heat of his close contact. "Why would you want to come to my defense?" she said. "I'm still that same pathetic fat slob I was back in high school. Nothing has changed. You heard what he called me."

Sebastian looked into her eyes. "You can't take anything that loser says to heart. He's a jerk. Why don't you go inside and change, then we can talk. If that's okay with you?"

Octavia lost the battle with her tears. "Don't come to me offering a lifeline. Pretending to care. I don't trust you. I don't trust anybody. No one ever stays. You'll get through my defenses and make me trust you and believe that you care for me, then you'll trick me too. You'll find some way to ridicule and mock me."

"I don't blame you for feeling the way you do," Sebastian whispered while moving closer. "It's hard to trust when you've been disappointed so many times you can't count." He put one hand on her shoulder and the other under her chin. "But you have to trust someone sometime, and I want to be that someone for you. Would you let me be the one? I promise I will try my best not to ever let you down."

Slowly, Sebastian wiped a tear from Octavia's cheek. Then he leaned in and touched his lips to the tear track. "I'm sorry about not being able to protect you when we were in high school, but we're different people now. I've learned to stand up for myself, and I think I can stand up for you, too, now. If you give me the chance."

When Octavia tried to look down, Sebastian wouldn't release her chin. He moved his other hand from her shoulder to the small of her back and pulled her closer to him. Leaning down to look into her eyes, he said, "You know, you're not the only one who's afraid of the world, don't you?"

Octavia looked into his sad, lonely eyes and was caught up in the tender emotion she saw. She shook her head. "I'm so afraid. I want to trust you, but . . ."

Sebastian wrapped both arms around her and held her tightly against his chest. "No buts," he said, "just say yes, and we'll take a journey toward faith, dependence, commitment, and reliance on one another, together."

Octavia returned the embrace and nodded her head.

"That's my girl," Sebastian said.

They held each other for a long time before he broke the embrace, stepped back, and kissed Octavia on the forehead. "Go inside and get some rest. We can talk another time."

Sebastian opened her sliding door and helped her step into the house. Then he closed the door and pointed to the lock and the security bar. When she had engaged both, he raised his hand in a goodbye wave, walked through the gate, and went into his house.

Stopping just inside his back door, Sebastian asked himself, *What am I thinking? I can't insinuate myself into that woman's life.*

He turned to look out the window of the door.

Man, she's going to require more time than you can imagine, he told himself, *but on the other hand, I think I'm ready to step outside of my box and trust somebody again. And she makes me want to take that step.*

CHAPTER 18
Thinking Back

S ebastian Warwick chuckled to himself.

"Trust," he whispered.

Sliding his hands into his side pockets, he thought, *Was it really just a year ago that my first meaningful relationship ended?* He smiled sadly and continued his introspection.

He turned from the door and walked into his den. He was thinking about Amara. Had it only been four months since she'd shown up at his door and demanded he come to his senses or lose her forever?

They met the summer he completed his masters of classical music and piano performance studies. She had attended his final thesis presentation performance, and when she at long last had the opportunity to congratulate him during the reception, they seemed to be instantly attracted to each other. For the next six years, they had maintained a close relationship.

Amara Watson was a beautiful woman who had overcome many obstacles in her life and was tired of working and fighting for everything she owned. She wanted to be taken care of, and Sebastian was her choice for providing her with that much-desired lifestyle.

She thought he owed her a life of luxury since she had been his girlfriend and companion through his long years of study for his Ph.D.

Now that Sebastian had several basic and advanced classical piano music books published, along with several original compositions that had been adopted by the music industry and deemed worthy of presentation by symphony orchestras, Amara felt she should be moved into a large house with servants where she would be treated like royalty.

She made it clear she was not happy when Sebastian informed her he was moving to Bothell, Washington, and that the house he was moving into was nowhere near the yuppie mansion she desired. Neither was it anything like the spacious suburban house he was raised in, but rather a moderately sized city cottage.

In the middle of her argument, Sebastian let her know he was not willing to be the one to provide the socialite lifestyle for her. Amara's reaction left a bitter afterthought, and he was more than pleased when she—loudly and rudely interrupting his mid-day practice session— stormed into his apartment, packed up her clothes and any gifts she had given him, threw his keys at him, and screamed, "I hate you! Go to Hell!"

Imagine his surprise when a few weeks after he had settled into his new home, Amara showed up on his doorstep. She was still beautiful. Her smile was almost captivating.

"Hello, darling," she said in her most proper French-African accent. "I've missed you. Aren't you going to invite me in? I've traveled a long way, you know."

Sebastian was more than surprised. "Who told you how to get here?" he asked her.

The frown on his face should have given Amara an indication she was not a welcomed guest, but if she noticed it, she paid no attention. Instead, she kept up her pretense of being happy to see him and to be at his home. As Sebastian stood in the entryway holding the door open, she took the opportunity to step inside.

"Silly," she said nonchalantly, "it was Jerrod, your agent. He purchased my ticket and even gave me this map. As a matter of fact, he said you would probably be more than glad to see me by now."

Because Amara was already inside, Sebastian closed the door. "What do you want? Didn't you say everything that you wanted to say when you threw my keys at me and directed me to go to Hell?"

Amara stepped close to him and put her arms around his neck. "Oh, come on, Hot Chocolate, you can't still be angry about that little incident. It meant nothing. I was just a little upset that you were relocating. You know I love New York, and I had never thought of us leaving it, especially to move this far away."

She pressed closer then tried to kiss him, but he turned his head, and her lips landed on his cheek. "I'm willing to forget what happened back there and try to live here if it makes you happy," Amara said. "Right now, I'm willing to say that I want whatever you want. I just want to be with you."

Sebastian removed her arms from his neck and stepped back. "Amara, we should have had this talk before I left New York. Then you wouldn't have had to come this far to be disappointed."

She looked somberly at him. "What are you trying to say, darling?"

He returned her phony, well-practiced gaze with one that was determined and unwavering. "I had no intention of bringing you here to live with me. I have long ago grown tired of your social-climbing antics. You are not the kind of woman I want to spend the rest of my life with. I want someone who is satisfied with who and what she is, and who accepts me for who and what I am. So I came back home to find someone I can spend the rest of my life with."

She looked at him with fire in her eyes. "What am I supposed to do now? Sebastian, you need to come to your senses or you're going to lose me forever. You can't do this to me. You owe me. I spent all those years with you, being your companion, and you think I'm going to disappear just like that? Let me tell you something, sunshine, I'm going to get you back for this. I'm going to get some compensation for putting my life on hold for you. You misled me and made me believe we had a future together."

Sebastian stepped to the front door and opened it wide. "No, let me tell you something, Amara. We were never officially living together because you maintained your own living space away from my apartment. You had your own means of income apart from mine, and your name was never on my mailbox. You have no grounds for a palimony case. So goodbye. I hope that you have a good flight back to your beloved New York."

When she walked out of the house, Amara turned to look at him. "My flight is not until Monday morning. Where am I supposed to stay until then?"

Sebastian smiled. "Because we did mean something to each other at one time, I'm going to call the airport Hilton and reserve a room for you. Goodbye, Amara."

With that said, he quietly closed the door in her face.

In spite of his outward appearance of being calm and in control, Sebastian was angry—so angry that he spent the next few hours playing out his frustration and anger on his piano. It wasn't until later that he thought about his next-door neighbor. He thought he should apologize, but it was past midnight, so he conditioned his hands and went to bed.

CHAPTER 19
Out with the Old, In with the New

The following week was a mix of bitter and sweet for Octavia. The bitter came every time she thought about Matthew—that lying, conniving, self-centered cheat. The sweet came every time she thought about Sebastian and the interaction they'd had in her back yard after the incident with Matthew.

Sebastian was an oasis of hope. He helped Octavia feel good about herself. He showed her that she didn't have to settle for someone to share her life with and that she had the right to be selective about whom she spent her life with.

On Monday, a large bouquet of roses was delivered to Octavia's office, along with a beautiful set of gold bangle bracelets. They were, of course, from Matthew. Also on Monday, she met Sebastian at the City Center Museum to tour James Van Der Zee's Harlem Renaissance exhibition.

On Tuesday, a large box of chocolates was delivered to her office, accompanied by a necklace that matched the bangle bracelets. Also on Tuesday, Sebastian and Octavia toured the Arts and Humanities buildings on campus and participated in a beginner's ballroom dance class.

Wednesday's delivery was a large teddy bear holding a smaller teddy bear holding a card that read *My Dearest Octavia, I'm sorry, please forgive me. Let's talk. Matthew.* Also on Wednesday, Octavia and Sebastian had a simple dinner together at a small bistro in mid-town.

Thursday morning dawned bright with a slight hint of autumn in the air. Octavia thought it was a perfect time to take out the enclosure for the pool. Thursday was her down day. She usually had one evening class, but tonight was the presidents' reception, and all evening classes had been canceled.

Just as she was setting the domed frame in place, Sebastian walked through the gate and caught Octavia off guard. "Do you need some help?" he asked.

Surprised, she turned, smiling. "As a matter of fact, I do."

For the next hour and a half, they worked on erecting the enclosure that ensured Octavia warm fall and winter swimming. When the dome was securely in place and the doors were zipped shut, Octavia's front doorbell rang. She ran through the house, opened the door, and directed the UPS driver to take a very large box from her living room to his truck. She paid him and ran back to the kitchen where Sebastian was standing, watching the exchange.

Octavia smiled. "Those were all of the gifts Matthew sent me this week. I boxed them, and I'm having them sent to his wife in his name."

Sebastian laughed robustly. "That's a very sophisticated thing to do, Miss Peterson." Then he stepped close to his next-door neighbor, looked down at her, leaned forward, and whispered in her ear, "You are an amazing woman. The more I'm around you, the more I want to be a part of your life."

Slowly, Octavia turned to look directly into Sebastian's compassionate, handsome face and the warm, deep-brown eyes with the longest, thickest eyelashes she had ever seen. Before she could say a word, tears began to roll down her cheeks. Sebastian gathered her to his chest. The two stood in full-body contact while Octavia cried on his chest.

Later on, at exactly 6:45, Octavia's front doorbell chimed. When she opened the door, she and Sebastian looked at each other and smiled broadly. Sebastian was dressed in a charcoal three-button long jacket evening suit. It looked very astute with the cranberry and silver vest and cranberry shirt, tie, and pocket-handkerchief. His dreadlocks were fresh and shiny, and tonight he was wearing them loosely so that they fell to his shoulders and framed his face.

Octavia was elegantly dressed in a one-shoulder black taffeta mid-length cocktail dress with a lace bolero jacket. Her hair was loose and cascaded down to her shoulders in a straw curl style.

Stepping inside to help her with her wrap, Sebastian gently cupped Octavia's face in his hands and lovingly touched his lips to hers. It wasn't his intention to make that move on her, but he couldn't help himself. She looked mesmerizing.

He took her hand, and as he was leading her out the door, he said, "You're going to be the most beautiful woman at the reception tonight."

CHAPTER 20
The Reception

Arriving at the reception hall was an intense experience for Octavia. She had always been uncomfortable being the center of attention, and as she and Sebastian walked into the Baldwin Reception Hall, they became just that: the center of attention.

She heard the intakes of breath that some made when they saw her companion. She also heard several people whisper, "That's Sebastian!" Others whispered, "Hey, isn't that Sebastian, the classical pianist?"

Trying not to draw too much attention to himself, Sebastian smiled and nodded his head but didn't stop to acknowledge anyone. As if he were aware of her discomfort, Sebastian stepped close, touched Octavia's elbow, and guided her to a table that had her name on a place card: *Professor O. Peterson & Guest.*

"You sit here, and I'll get us some wine," Sebastian said softly to Octavia.

"That certainly is a handsome man," the woman next to Octavia said. When Octavia looked at her, the woman asked, "Is he your boyfriend?" She was nice-looking but seemed not to smile much. There was a sadness to her eyes that no smile could have touched. It seemed to be a part of her countenance.

"Almost," Octavia said. "But for right now, he's my knight in shining armor."

The lady touched Octavia's arm and leaned toward her. "I used to feel that way about someone once." Then she sat up straight, patted Octavia's arm, and added, "Hold on to that feeling for as long as you can. It's a good place to be."

The woman, who was probably no more than three or four years older than Octavia, excused herself and left the table.

When Sebastian didn't return right away, Octavia turned to look around the ballroom. She saw a small crowd of people standing by the bar, and then she saw Sebastian in the middle of the crowd. He was signing autographs. He looked up and caught her eye. He smiled and winked at her, then he excused himself from the crowd, picked up two goblets of wine, and walked across the floor.

Still smiling, he said, "I apologize for taking so long to get back, but I see you've been making friends already."

When Octavia looked at her handsome, caring, and considerate date, she had a distressing look in her eyes. Seeing her apparent sadness, Sebastian reached over and took her hands in his.

"What's the matter?" he asked.

Octavia replied, "That woman is so sweet and friendly. We just had a quick conversation about the men in our lives." When Sebastian asked why the conversation made Octavia sad, she told him, "Because the lady is Mrs. Matthew Edwards."

Shortly after that, Myrna Edwards returned to the table with her own glass of wine and a friendly greeting for Sebastian. Matthew walked pompously through the doors into the reception hall and stood looking around the room just to see if he was being noticed. As he did, he saw something that almost made him stop breathing: Octavia Peterson, that piano guy, and his wife Myrna were sitting at the same table, engaged in a conversation.

When Matthew saw his wife talking to Octavia, he grew furious. He wanted to stalk over to the table and snatch Octavia by the arm, drag her to the terrace, and give her a hard slap. But she was with that piano player, and Matthew didn't want to tangle with him again—not just yet, anyway.

So he fixed a big smile on his face and walked to the table. "Good evening, everyone. Professor Peterson," he said, nodding to Octavia, "how nice to see you here this evening."

Octavia looked at Matthew. "Hello, Professor Edwards, have you met my guest, Sebastian Warwick?"

Matthew sidestepped his wife's chair and shook Sebastian's hand. Trying to show an air of bravado, Matthew exerted a little pressure with his handshake, which was immediately met by even more forceful pressure from Sebastian. The two men looked at each other and released their grasp without exchanging a greeting.

Just as Matthew was sitting down next to his wife, the university president, Dr. Marcus Barrett, stepped to the front of the room, welcomed the faculty and staff and their family members, thanked them for coming to the reception, offered a prayer, and asked that dinner be served.

Myrna sensed she had once again done something to make her husband upset, but tonight she didn't care. She was tired of being the string on Matthew's emotional yo-yo. She wasn't going to let him keep her from enjoying this reception. She liked the lady who was sitting across from her, and so Myrna continued to engage in pleasant conversation with Octavia and Sebastian throughout the entire meal— and, as if adding more fuel to the fire, the two women continued their friendly chatter throughout the duration of the program that followed the meal.

When the musicians took the stage, Sebastian immediately asked Octavia to dance. Once on the dance floor, he held her in a light traditional embrace. She placed one of her hands gently on his arm, the other lightly on his shoulder, and looked up into his handsome face. They smiled at one another serenely and swayed to the rhythm of the music.

Before the song was over, Sebastian stepped away from Octavia, took her by the hand, and led her to the veranda that overlooked the garden. They stood on the terrace side by side and enjoyed the moonlight shining on the plants and trees. They also enjoyed each other's company. Even though they spoke no words to one another, this was a bonding moment for them both.

Octavia felt comfortable standing next to Sebastian, a man she had known in his teen years as a shy, withdrawn, unhappy boy. And now here he was: a full-grown, extremely handsome, self-assured, successful and talented man.

Sebastian was amazed by the fact that he was standing next to the one person in his life who had never judged him. His intuition told him Octavia was not the type to condemn or criticize others. He remembered from high school those few times they'd crossed paths that she had always had something positive to offer.

Slowly, Sebastian moved to stand behind Octavia and wrapped his arms around her. She was warm, she smelled good, and she felt like a perfect fit. The best part of this whole moment was when she accepted his embrace, relaxed, and leaned her head back to rest on his shoulder.

When the band began, Matthew didn't bother to ask. He stood and grabbed his wife's arm and almost dragged her to the dance floor. "Just what were you doing this evening?" he said through gritted teeth. "You never miss an opportunity to embarrass me, do you? You have no class. I don't know why I ever take you anywhere."

Without warning, Myrna stepped closer to her husband and hissed through gritted teeth, "Shut up, Matthew. That's right, I said shut up." She stepped back to look into his face. "You think I don't know what's going on?" She plastered a synthetic smile on her face. "I have put up with you and your disgusting ways for too long. I'm running this show now, and you're going to take it. Don't think I don't mean what I'm saying. You try to treat me harshly and callously one more time, and I'll tell President Barrett the real reason we had to leave the last university, and the one before that, and the one before that."

CHAPTER 21
Reset

Matthew's face fell. He looked at his wife with wide eyes. She knew she had his attention now. She also had the upper hand. His body stiffened, and he began to perspire profusely.

"Okay, baby, now, now, you just settle down a little bit. Let's not get carried away with these wild thoughts." Matthew's mind was whirling.

Does she really know, or is she just bluffing? he asked himself.

Placing another one of his fake smiles on his face, Matthew said to his wife, "Uh, sweetie, you . . . you know we moved here because it's affording us a better lifestyle and better benefits than our last school. That's why we're here. You know that, baby."

Myrna flashed him another disingenuous smile. "You can stop trying to placate me with your phony charms. They don't work on me. I know you, and I know what you've been doing. So shut up and straighten up your act, mister, or you're going to be back on the wrong side of the tracks in that little one-horse town you came from quicker than the blink of an eye."

For the rest of the song, Matthew stiffly and silently danced with his wife. He was beginning to feel sick; he felt like someone had punched him in his stomach; he couldn't breathe. When the song ended, he made his way back to the table. As soon as he was seated, he grabbed a glass of water and drank it almost in one gulp. He used the napkin to wipe his damp face.

Myrna sat down in the chair beside him and touched his hand. "It's okay, Matthew, don't fret. I'm giving you a second chance. You just remember that you have no margin for error. One slip-up and everything is gone, because as quiet as you've tried to keep it, we both know I'm the one with the money, and you're the great pretender."

She patted his hand and sat with him for the rest of the next song. When Octavia and Sebastian returned to the table, Myrna continued her small talk with her new friend. Then she asked Octavia to join her in the restroom. Once there, Myrna asked, "Professor Peterson, can we talk?"

Octavia looked at this woman who, under different circumstances, could be a good friend. "Of course, Mrs. Edwards. I think we have a lot to talk about."

"Professor Peterson," Myrna said, "I know who you are, and I know about your relationship with my husband."

When Octavia made no attempt to say anything, Myrna smiled.

"I like you, Professor Peterson. You are, as far as I can tell, an amazing woman. No wonder Matthew was attracted to you. But I believe with you he bit off more than he could chew. You are nothing like he thought you would be: sad, lonely, and gullible."

Taking Octavia's hands in hers, Myrna looked into Octavia's eyes.

"You said earlier this evening that Sebastian was your knight in shining armor. Well, I want you to let yourself trust him and let yourself fall in love with him because he's already in love with you." A tear slid slowly down Myrna's cheek. "I loved my husband once. I thought of him as my knight in shining armor, too, until I realized that he is, in all probability, not capable of loving anyone but himself. And for that, I feel sorry for him, but we are married and I don't believe in divorce, so I want you to know that I don't hold you responsible for what happened between you and him. All I ask is that you have nothing else to do with him."

Octavia leaned forward and hugged Myrna. "May I share some things with you, Mrs. Edwards? I'd like to clear the air between us."

The two women looked at each other, then after some time, Myrna nodded her head and whispered, "Yes."

"The relationship between Matthew and I was never physical beyond a kiss. We met at an anniversary party I gave my parents at my home. Matthew was new to the faculty, and my father invited him just to keep him from spending the weekend alone in a new city."

Octavia stopped and offered Myrna a few tissues. Then she continued sharing the information about how the relationship had developed. She told Myrna how she and Matthew would sometimes meet for lunch and how they would mostly meet at the gym for workout sessions. She told her about the few meals she had cooked for him at her home, but she reassured Myrna that nothing physical happened. Finally, Octavia told Myrna how Matthew began to get possessive and domineering.

"And for me, that was too much too soon," Octavia said sadly. "Then my parents told me Matthew was married, and that while I was away on a trip, you and the children had moved into his house. When I let him know I was no longer interested in pursuing a relationship, he became aggressive. That's where my knight comes in. Sebastian heard Matthew being hostile, disrespectful, and belligerent. He stepped in and, let's say, persuaded Matthew to leave me alone by flipping him into my swimming pool."

Myrna laughed unhappily. "That must have been the day he came home soaking wet and said that the sprinkler system at the school had come on just as he was crossing the campus lawn heading toward his car."

The women sat holding hands for a while longer. Eventually, they both dried their eyes, stood, repaired their makeup, and just as they were about to walk out of the restroom, Myrna said, "Thank you, Professor Peterson."

When the ladies returned to the table, Matthew was sitting alone. He stood and stared at both women questioningly. He looked like a little boy who had just been caught with his hands in the cookie jar.

Sebastian returned to the table and led Octavia to the dance floor again. "So how did it go? Neither one of you looks like any blood was spilled. What happened?"

Octavia smiled and said, "I told her you were my knight in shining armor, and she told me to hold on to that feeling for as long as I can."

Sebastian looked at Octavia. "Really? A knight in shining armor?" He smiled. "I like that."

CHAPTER 22
The Real Thing

Sebastian pulled his car into Octavia's driveway. He exited his side of the car, opened her door, and offered his hand to help her out of the car. He continued to hold her hand as they walked to her front door.

When he took her key and opened the door, he asked, "Do you mind if I check the house?"

She shook her head slowly and waited for him to come back.

"It's all clear, Miss Peterson, you are safe to enter now," he said with a smile. Then, without thinking, when he handed Octavia her key, he unhurriedly embraced her and kissed her softly and gently.

Just as he was breaking contact, Sebastian whispered, "I hope that when you cried on my shoulder this afternoon, it meant you've let go of your relationship with Matthew." He reluctantly released his hold on Octavia. "Good night, neighbor."

Before she could respond, he got back into his car and backed out of her driveway. Octavia stepped into her entryway, closed the door, leaned against it, and sighed.

When she had finished her shower and was brushing her hair, Octavia heard a sweet, enchanting melody coming from Sebastian's house. She climbed onto her bed and laid on her side, hugging a pillow, listening to the most beautiful sound she had ever heard.

Sebastian played his piano until two o'clock in the morning. He kept asking himself the same question over and over: *Am I ready to start a new relationship?*

Then he asked himself, *Will she want to have a relationship with me?*

Finally, sleep began to descend on him, and he laid down for a nap. He had a late flight out on Friday night, and he wanted to talk with Octavia before he left.

Octavia had two early-morning classes on Friday and one hour of scheduled office time, so it was one o'clock before she got back home. When she pulled into the driveway, Sebastian was sitting on her front porch.

"Now that certainly is one good-looking man!" she said to herself.

Instead of driving into the garage, she parked in the driveway and walked to her porch to sit next to her visitor.

"Well, hello. This is a surprise. What can I do for you this afternoon, Mr. Warwick?"

Sebastian looked at Octavia and gave her a dazzling smile. "I didn't keep you from sleeping last night, did I?"

She returned his smile and said simply, "No."

Sebastian stood and walked to the opposite end of the porch and back again to stand in front of Octavia. He looked down at her. "I believe that I want to have a relationship with you. Are you ready to get involved again so soon after . . . you know . . . or should I just go away and leave you alone?"

Octavia stood and slid her arms around Sebastian's waist. "I don't think you should just leave me alone, Mr. Warwick, because I'm interested in a relationship with you."

When she said that, Sebastian threw his arms around Octavia and kissed her until they both were out of breath.

They spent the rest of the afternoon together. He took her to lunch, and they went to the city center park to sit in the sun and watch the ducks on the pond.

When they returned home, Sebastian kissed her again and said, "I have to leave tonight. I'll be gone for two weeks. When I get back, I'm going to cook you that amazing meal I promised you."

He kissed her again, watched her walk into her house, and then he sauntered across the lawn to his house.

CHAPTER 23
The Final Goodbye

At exactly ten o'clock Saturday morning, Octavia was having her second cup of tea when her doorbell rang. It was the florist, and he was delivering three dozen roses, each in separate containers.

"Good morning, are you Miss Peterson? Can you sign here, please?"

The phone rang as soon as the truck pulled out of her driveway. "Hello," she said cheerfully.

"You sound happy this morning," Sebastian said with a smile to his voice. "I'm calling my good-luck charm to see if she likes her early-morning surprise."

She was so happy that she couldn't stop smiling. "Yes, Mr. Warwick, I love my surprise, but why so many?"

"So you can put them in different rooms and feel like I'm right there with you."

"You are so sweet. Thank you, I love them."

"I have to go. I have a matinee concert in a couple of hours."

"Goodbye," Octavia said. "Have an exceptional concert."

"Goodbye, my good-luck charm."

Octavia was smiling as she took one bouquet to her bedroom, then placed another one in the middle of her kitchen table. The last vase she put on her desk in the den. She spent the rest of the weekend feeling happy and lonely at the same time.

When her phone rang for the second time that morning, Octavia quickly answered it, but when she heard Matthew's voice on the other end, she promptly hung up. When he called again, she didn't answer at all, and when he left messages, she erased them without listening to what he had to say.

Octavia's final friendly conversation with Matthew happened on Monday afternoon during her office hours. He ambled through her office door and sat across from her. "We need to have a serious conversation, Octavia, and since you won't answer my calls, it has to be here, unless you want to have a late lunch with me."

"Matthew, we have nothing to talk about. So please leave," she said to him sternly.

"We have lots to discuss, Octavia, and what if I don't want to leave? What are you going to do about it? That piano jockey isn't here, so how are you going to make me leave?" He crossed his arms and looked at her smugly.

She held up her cell phone. "I have your wife's cell number on speed dial. One push and she'll get a call from me."

Matthew dropped his arms and looked at Octavia with hatred in his eyes. "You are a vindictive, hateful person, Octavia Peterson. I don't know what I ever saw in you."

"We both know it's not what you saw in me, Matthew. It's what you thought you were going to get from me. So please leave, and let's agree to this being the last personal conversation we will ever have again." She smiled at him as he was walking out of the door. "Goodbye, Matthew."

By 9:30 that night when Octavia had completed her last lecture for the day, she walked to her car and found that all of her tires had been slashed. For a moment, she panicked. The campus was dark, and she was parked in an isolated area of the parking lot.

"Get a grip, girl, you're going to be okay," she said to herself. "This is not a problem. Just calm down and . . ."

She heard a car drive onto the lot and stop behind her. A voice called out laughingly, "Do you need a ride?"

She didn't turn around to acknowledge Matthew. She simply took out her cell phone and dialed a number. She heard him put his car in gear and turned to watch him drive quickly off of the lot and speed down the street. When her insurance hotline assistant answered, she reported the problem and waited for the tow truck and the rental car that was delivered to her.

When she was finally home and waiting for Sebastian to call, she resolved not to tell him about what had just happened. When they talked, it was about how the concert went and where his next performance would be.

Sebastian was excited as he told Octavia that his performance had been described as one of the best of his career by the music critics. He was so upbeat that she could hear the exhilaration in his voice.

"Listen to this. It's from Frederick Umbanger," he said, reading from the article. "*Sebastian was in rare form last night, and if you missed it, you missed the performance of a lifetime.* Then he added this: *Congratulations, Sebastian, you have arrived!*"

He told Octavia that in the past, this particular critic had said he was too young and inexperienced in life to be an outstanding classical stage concert performer.

"That's why I know that you are my good-luck charm, Professor Peterson," he said jokingly. "All I have to do is hear your voice, and my heart is happy, and my hands take on a life of their own. You're good for me, Octavia. I love you."

As soon as the words left his mouth, he thought, *Slow your roll, brother, this is too much too soon.*

For several moments, neither of them said anything.

"You didn't hang up on me, did you?" Sebastian finally said softly into the phone.

Octavia took a deep breath. "No, I didn't hang up. I'm just surprised. No one has ever said that to me before. Say it again, please."

"Well, I wanted to say it to you in person, but I'm falling in love with you, Octavia. I think I have been falling in love with you since high school." Again, there was silence on the line. Sebastian spoke soothingly, "I know you're crying, and I wish I could be there to hold you. I didn't mean to upset you. Forgive me for being so thoughtless."

Through her tears, Octavia managed to say, "I'm so happy to hear you say those words that I just don't know what to say. Except that I think I love you too. And I still consider you my knight in shining armor. When are you coming home?"

"I'll be home in twelve days," he reported. "I have five more concerts, then I'll be back, and I want you to be the first thing I see when I get off the plane. I'll make sure you get the flight information a couple of days before I'm due to arrive so you can meet me at the airport."

"If you send me the information, I'll be there. Nothing could stop me from being there," Octavia said, trying to smile. "Good night, Sebastian."

CHAPTER 24
It's Real Love

When she arrived on campus the next morning, Octavia went directly to the security office and reported what had happened to her car. She was immediately given an assigned parking stall in a secured area and was assured her car would be safe.

When her classes were over, Octavia went to her office and called Mom and Pop Harrington's house. When Mom answered, Octavia asked if she could have dinner with them.

"Of course you can have dinner with us, little girl," Mom Harrington said. Then she asked, "What's wrong, are you alright?"

"Mom, why does something have to be wrong for me to come see you?" They both chuckled, and Octavia said, "I'll be there in an hour."

When Pop Harrington arrived home, he asked Octavia why she was driving a rental car and was highly upset when she reported what had happened to her car.

"Do you have any idea who it could have been?" he asked.

"I'll tell you who I think it was, even though I can't prove it, if you promise not to get upset or try to do something about it. I want to handle it myself." She looked back and forth at both of her adopted parents. When they nodded their heads, she said, "I think it was Matthew Edwards."

"Matthew Edwards, really? Why do you think it was him?" Mom Harrington asked.

Octavia told Mom and Pop Harrington about the incidents that had taken place, from the time Matthew began to show his true colors to the incident in her back yard to his appearance in her office yesterday afternoon, and finally his comment in the parking lot the night before.

"How are you going to handle it?" Pop Harrington asked.

"I don't know yet. But I'm hoping he'll get the picture that I want to have nothing to do with him ever again. And maybe I won't have to do anything major."

"Why would he do something so shameful and wicked?" Mom Harrington said. "I think you should call the police. He sounds like a madman."

In order to change the subject, Octavia said, "I think I'm in love."

They looked at her in wonderment. Then they looked at each other and back at the young lady they had both grown to love and regard as their own daughter. Grinning broadly, they waited for Octavia to expound on her announcement.

Pop Harrington immediately went into Daddy mode. "Who is it?"

"His name is Sebastian Warwick," Octavia replied with a smile. "We went to high school together, and after his graduation, we lost contact with one another. Now he's back, and he's my next-door neighbor. The one who came to my rescue from Matthew."

"As in Sebastian, the concert pianist?" Pop Harrington asked excitedly.

"Yes, Pop. Once you all meet, I think you and Mom will love him as much as I do. We have so much in common, and he is a very down-to-earth, kind, and considerate gentleman."

Mom Harrington stood, walked around the table, and hugged Octavia. "Oh, baby, I'm so happy for you."

On Wednesday evening, as she was undressing after work, Octavia's phone rang. "Hello?" she answered.

"Hello yourself," Sebastian said. "You know that I had to call you just to hear your voice. I couldn't call yesterday because we were traveling, and then there was a late practice. So I'm calling you tonight just before my concert is about to start."

Sebastian paused, then he said, "Octavia, I want to tell you that Monday night's performance was recorded for a CD, and I'm sending you a copy. When you get it, I want you to listen to the selection titled 'Beauty.' I composed it with you in mind even before we met again. It was you I had in mind. I just didn't know it at the time."

His comment took her by complete surprise.

"And, Octavia, I dedicated the selection to you during the concert."

Octavia heard Sebastian laugh out loud. It was such a captivatingly rich sound, and it made her smile. Then he said, "I hope you like it. Good night, my good-luck charm."

Octavia was so happy. This was the first time in her life that she had even thought she could have a real relationship with someone she could trust, especially with someone so high-profile as Sebastian Warwick.

As she thought back to their high school days, Octavia reminded herself that even back then, she thought he was a nice-looking young man. But she never imagined he would have grown into the handsome, appealing man he was now. She also never imagined they would be back in each other's lives embarking on a relationship, especially after so many years.

CHAPTER 25
Deceiving Appearances

Sebastian Warwick's appearance gave the impression that he was an outgoing, sociable man about town. He was tall, a little taller than average, very physically fit, and his clothes looked like they had been tailored just for him. His dreadlocked hair was always neat with a sharp, fresh line-up. His face was clean-shaven with a thin, trimmed mustache.

He manifested an always in control, self-assured, in-charge demeanor. All of that had helped him move forward in his career. He had become a master at hiding his true feelings and internal uncertainties. He had never told anyone that he suffered from anxiety attacks that sometimes led to bouts of depression. All of the unsettled feelings in his life could be attributed to his early home life.

Sebastian knew in the back of his mind that something had to be done about his relationship with his parents, especially his father. He had not had any real contact with either of his parents for fifteen years.

He did, however, keep informed about them and their well-being by calling his sister, Natalia, and asking how they were. In the past, he would send his mother flowers on her birthday. Until Natalia told him that their father had forbidden their mother from bringing anything from her rebellious, ungrateful, disobedient son into his house. So

Sebastian would have them delivered to his Natalia's house, and Natalia would take them to their mother.

Sebastian was tired of this disconnect. He was tired of living like an orphan. He felt there was no way he could get seriously involved with someone like Octavia Peterson if his personal life was dysfunctional.

He had become so good at wearing that mask of self-confidence that even his closest associates didn't know he was sad, lonely, and unhappy most of the time. No one had ever known of his deep desire to prove to his parents, especially his father, that he was not a failure. He wanted his parents to be proud of him and to accept the fact that even though he didn't become an engineer like they wanted, he was happy as an entertainer. Now it appeared that after this concert tour, he was finally going to be recognized as a success in his field.

"Nine performances down, three to go," Sebastian said to himself, "then I'll see her again."

Having Octavia in his life had been a good thing for him. Since he'd been with her, his depression and insecurities had been minimal. He thought about Octavia and her unconditional acceptance of him.

When she looks at me, I don't see disappointment or disapproval in her eyes. She even calls me her knight in shining armor, and I don't ever want to do anything to tarnish her vision of me.

Octavia hadn't heard from Sebastian in two days, and she wanted desperately to hear his voice. She did receive the live performance CD and immediately listened to it. She was amazed by how he used his talent and his skill of playing to draw real emotions from the listener.

When she listened to the selection entitled "Beauty," it was a magical experience. She enjoyed his skillful flair for blending notes into an arrangement that was delightfully enthralling, velvety smooth, and undeniably mesmerizing.

She thought to herself, *He's a musical genius, and he says he loves me!* Her smile was so bright that she felt like she was glowing.

CHAPTER 26
The Payback

O ctavia didn't have much time before Sebastian returned, and she wanted to get the situation with Matthew settled before his homecoming. She had a plan and hoped it would be accepted by everyone involved.

The first thing Octavia did was to invite Myrna Edwards to breakfast in the cafeteria on Thursday morning. After they got their food and were seated, Octavia told Myna that there was a job on campus she thought would be perfect for her. When Octavia showed Myrna the job description and qualifications, Myrna left her partially eaten breakfast on the table and went directly to the human resources office to apply.

The director of human resources gladly met with Myrna. He told her it was reported to him that she had an M.S. in physical fitness and dance and that she had come highly recommended. If she wanted the position, it was hers for the taking.

Myrna was happy to have a job and even more pleased to discover it was Octavia who had recommended her. She was hired and assigned to the physical education department on campus. Myrna's position was as a dance teacher in the Fitness for Life program.

After signing her contract and completing her personnel packet,

Myrna went to Octavia's office. She knocked on the door, and when Octavia said, "Come in, please," the newest teacher on campus walked in and hugged her.

"Professor Peterson," Myrna said, "I don't know how I will ever be able to thank you for all you've done for me. I've always wanted to use my training, and since you recommended me, I'm now going to be earning a paycheck on my own with my name on it. Thank you."

She reached out and hugged Octavia again, and then she stepped back. The two women looked at each other. "I think under different circumstances," Myrna added, "we could have been great friends."

Octavia grabbed Myrna's shoulders. "Mrs. Edwards, I think being colleagues and associates is almost as good as being friends."

As she was leaving the campus, Octavia felt pleased with herself. She knew the last thing Matthew wanted was for his wife to have a job, especially one on the same campus where he was teaching. Octavia felt she had paid him back royally for slashing her tires. Now all she had to do was wait for the other shoe to fall, and that would be pretty soon—especially if she had read Matthew correctly.

Octavia was proud of the fact she didn't have to do something as childish and pathetic as Matthew had done. She was glad this was something positive for someone else. She knew Myrna was not as happy with her life as she could have been, and Octavia simply thought that if Myrna could get out of the house on a regular basis and into a situation where Matthew was not able to control her every thought and movement, maybe she would be a happier person.

After returning the rental car and picking up her own, Octavia thought to herself, *I only wish I could be a fly on the wall when he finds out his wife is now an employee of the college.*

The next morning as she arrived at work, Octavia was parking her car in her assigned space on the secured lot when Matthew stopped short behind her. He jumped out of his car and confronted her.

"You heifer, how dare you interfere in my personal life? You had no right to encourage my wife to get a job! I'll get you back for this.

You can count on it. And this time, it's going to be more than slashing your tires. That's right—it was me, and you'd better watch out."

Opening her car door and stepping out, Octavia smiled and said, "You don't scare me, Matthew, and I don't think you're going to do anything to me because you've just confessed to committing a crime. If I choose to, I can press charges, and your career will be over."

She smiled at him, held up her cell phone, and replayed his confession. Then she pointed to something behind him. When he turned around, Matthew looked directly into the face of the chief of campus security.

"What can we do for you today, Professor Edwards?" the taller, excessively muscular man smilingly asked.

Matthew was stunned to find himself in such a position. *I should have seen this coming,* he thought. *She's such a bitter woman that she would never give a real man a chance.*

He turned to look at Octavia and then back to the chief. "I'm not sure I know what you're talking about, Officer," Matthew said in his most persuasive manner.

The chief looked the professor up and down then leaned forward and said, "Now listen up, *Mr.* Edwards, I'm pretty sure you don't want to follow through on your threat. I'm also pretty sure you don't want us to go to Dr. Barrett *and* the city police with your confession. So tell me, what do you plan to do to get this situation taken care of?"

Doing some quick talking and making somber promises, Matthew agreed to pay Octavia for the replacement of her tires and to cover all expenses related to the incident. He also promised he would not have any contact with Octavia, on or off campus, again.

"Good," the chief said, "because we have those promises recorded also. So be a good man and leave this woman alone. And now you should get back in your car and get off this lot. It's restricted. You have to have a pass to park here."

Looking somewhat defeated, Matthew quickly re-entered his car and drove away, leaving the chief and Octavia feeling as though they'd accomplished something.

"Alright, Professor Peterson, let's go to my office and transfer that information onto my computer," he said as he offered his arm and escorted her into the campus security building.

CHAPTER 27
Apart

The rest of the week went by pleasantly for Octavia. She didn't see Matthew anywhere on the campus, but she did see Myrna, and each time they saw one other, they exchanged smiles and friendly greetings.

Evenings for Octavia were quiet. She received a phone call on the following Wednesday after prayer service. It was Sebastian.

"Hello, Octavia."

"Hello yourself," she said. "How are you, and how did last night's concert go? Where are you calling from? Aren't you traveling?"

Sebastian laughed. "So many questions. Well, to start, I'm fine now that I hear your voice. The concert was outstanding. We received more positive first-rate reviews. Now tell me what you've been doing since I've been gone."

For just a moment, Octavia had a passing wave of anxiety, but she quickly recovered. "I've just been going to work every day and visiting my parents. But most of all, I've been coming home waiting to hear from you." The line went silent for a few moments. "Sebastian? Are you still there?"

"Yes," he said. "I have something to tell you . . . and I don't know how to say it."

"Why don't you start from the beginning, and maybe we can isolate the problem and perhaps even find a solution to it?"

Sebastian took a deep breath and released it slowly. "I really think I should say it in person. I need to be looking in your face when we have this conversation."

Octavia could hear something in his voice but couldn't identify it. "Well, there are just two more concerts, and the tour will be over. Isn't that right? So don't think about whatever it is right now. Just focus on your performances, and we'll talk about it when you get here. Can it wait that long?"

Sebastian gave a mirthless chuckle. "It's waited this long. I guess a few more days won't really matter."

"Sebastian," Octavia said, "I've never met anyone as disciplined, focused, and confident as you. Whatever it is that you want to talk about must be heavy-duty, but I want to promise you that I won't think any differently about you than I do now, whatever it is you have to tell me."

Again, there was a long pause in the conversation and she thought the connection had been severed, but Sebastian finally said, "That's why I'm falling in love with you, Miss Peterson. You always know just what to say."

"You make it easy to love you, Mr. Warwick," Octavia softly said.

"And that's another reason why you're my good-luck charm. You make me feel like I'm really important to you."

"You are important to me, Sebastian. You've brought light into what has previously been a very dark life," Octavia said.

The next thing that Sebastian said to Octavia was, "You should go to sleep now, and I will call you tomorrow. Good night."

He didn't wait for her response; he severed the connection before he could say anything else to her. He envisioned her as pure, innocent, and inexperienced, and she made him feel so special that he didn't want to hide any part of his life from her.

Talking to himself, Sebastian said, "I certainly hope you meant what you said, Miss Peterson, because we have a lot to talk about."

He walked across the room to the baby grand piano by the window in the hotel penthouse suite. Without thinking, he began to play "Beauty." It reminded him of Octavia, the first person outside of his family he had probably ever loved who loved him back.

CHAPTER 28
Something's Wrong

Just as he promised, Sebastian called Octavia again the next night. However, it was later than he usually called.

"Hello," she whispered groggily.

"I knew it was too late to call you," he said. "Go back to sleep and we'll talk in the morning."

Octavia sat up and turned on the bedside lamp. "No, please don't hang up. I've been waiting all day to hear your voice."

"You have? Why? Is something wrong?" he asked, sounding concerned.

"No, nothing is wrong. I just miss you, and I'm so excited about your being home in a couple of days."

"Oh, well, then I'm glad I called. What was your day like?"

"It was a day like any other day," she said. "I lectured, went to my office between classes, graded papers, and hurried home so I wouldn't miss your call."

"Okay, that certainly is routine," he said.

Sebastian was a little on edge, and Octavia could hear it in his voice. "Sebastian, you sound different. Is something wrong?"

Hesitantly, he replied, "Well, there is something I wanted to talk to you about. Octavia, I'm going to be coming home a few days later than

I expected. I have some business that needs to be taken care of before I get there. You don't mind, do you?"

"Of course I don't mind. Whatever it is, you should take care of it. I'll see you when you get here."

Trying to lighten the mood of the conversation, Octavia said, "You should know that I'm really proud of you, and I'm really happy you're finally being recognized for your hard work. Nobody deserves the appreciation and respect more than you do. It's time, actually past time, that the world finds out about a wonderful, talented musician like you."

"Octavia," Sebastian said, "I think you may have a few unrealistic ideas about me, and I need to dispel them before we go deeper into our relationship. But first, I have to ask . . . Are you interested in being in a lasting relationship with me?"

Smiling, she replied, "Do you mean to tell me that we're not in a relationship yet?" She laughed quietly and continued. "I probably wouldn't consider you my knight in shining armor if we weren't in a relationship, Mr. Warwick."

"Well, I have to tell you that my armor has a few chinks in it," Sebastian said lightly. "I haven't exactly spent one hundred percent of my time playing the piano. There are some things about me and some people who have been in my life that you should know about."

"Everybody has a past, Sebastian. I'm not interested in your past. I'm more concerned about your present and your future, as long as it involves us being together in a stable, secure, mutually respectful relationship."

Sebastian replied, "There was a time in my recent past when I would not have initiated a relationship with someone like you. You're so comfortable and content with yourself in spite of your earlier childhood distresses. How did you get to where you are now?"

Softly and thoughtfully, Octavia said, "There comes a time when you get tired of running and realize that you have to face your demons. So that's what I did. I faced my demons. I started losing weight. I followed my dream and began writing. I eliminated everything from my life that held me prisoner to my past. Basically, I guess you could say that I got myself a new attitude. It took a lot of prayer, faith, and determination."

"Well, good for you," he said. "Some things in life can't be resolved with that mind-over-matter stuff. Some things go so deep that they can't be forgotten."

He seemed to be fighting a personal battle. He was in the midst of one of his anger storms, and she could hear an agitation and tension in his voice.

"Octavia, I have to go. I'll call you in a few hours."

Instead of letting the conversation end, Octavia quickly said, "Sebastian, wait!" When he made no comment, Octavia said, "Whatever it is that you're holding onto from your past, you have to let it go. You have to see it as something that you have overcome. You have to know that God has brought you through something that you thought was overwhelming and devastating. You have to see yourself as triumphant because you are. You have been blessed to survive, and whatever it is or whoever it is that you're allowing to define you—face it, forgive and forget it. If you don't, you'll always be a prisoner to it or to them. I don't know about you, but personally, I don't want anything or anyone to have that kind of control and power over me but God."

When she finished, Sebastian said, "Good night, Octavia," and quickly hung up the phone.

CHAPTER 29
Face It

After his conversation with Octavia, Sebastian sat in his hotel room and cried tears of frustration and anger. He was so angry he couldn't even find peace in his playing. He kept hearing Octavia's voice say, "Face it, forgive and forget it . . ."

He had to admit that he needed to face some things in his life. There was something that had been hanging over his head for too long, and Octavia was probably right. If he wanted some peace, if he wanted to be free from his past, he needed to face his adversary, that one person whose approval he had sought all of his life but was denied.

Again, he heard the sweet voice of the woman he was afraid he was falling in love with. "See yourself as triumphant . . . face it, forgive and forget it . . ."

This has been hanging over my head long enough, he thought to himself. *I can't be free until I get this situation straightened out.*

It had been fifteen years since Sebastian had been inside his parents' home or had any personal contact with them. He remembered his father's words to him the day he left for Julliard: "Since you are so defiant and headstrong and you won't do what I told you to do, there is no need for you to ever come back to this house again. Not unless you change your mind and start doing what I've said you should do.

And that is to go to a real school and prepare yourself for a real career."

Even with that said, his father was not finished with his barrage of degrading and hateful words.

"I don't know why I'm wasting my words on the likes of you. You've never been the kind of son a man could be proud of anyway. You're a fat slob, you're soft, and I have no use for you."

The words had felt like a stab in the heart. For most of his life, Sebastian knew he was different, that he didn't fall in line like his other siblings even though he had tried to do whatever he could to please his father. But time after time, it seemed nothing he did was ever good enough. By the time he was fifteen, he had stopped trying to please the senior Mr. Warwick.

Instead of rushing through his afterschool piano lessons, Sebastian stayed for hours and often practiced until his hands were sore. When he was asked where he had been, he was honest and straightforward. He said he had been taking lessons. Practicing. Writing music. Anything music-related that he knew would anger his father.

Usually, as a result, his father would hit or berate him, and Sebastian would endure it. Until his eighteenth birthday when his father tried to hit him and Sebastian seized the belt. He would have struck his father with it if his mother had not intervened.

Two days after that incident, Sebastian graduated from high school as Valedictorian, a regional sterling scholar in music and recipient of a full-ride scholarship to the Julliard School of Music.

Even to the very last minute, as he was celebrating his accomplishments, Sebastian's father was relentless in his criticism. Nathaniel Warwick's parting words to his son were, "If you go to that music school, don't bother to come back here. No son of mine is going to make a living as some juke-joint cigar-bar piano player. In my day, children did what they were told and didn't disrespect their parents by going against their wishes."

Twenty-four hours later, Sebastian was on an airplane headed for New York City. Those words had been in his mind for fifteen years.

But that was the past. Sebastian was on a mission, and he was determined to walk away feeling like his mission had been accomplished. So when he arrived at his parents' house, Sebastian had the limo driver let him out at the base of their driveway. He stood looking at the house he grew up in for a few minutes with one hand in his pocket. In his other hand, he held a book.

It's funny, he thought to himself, *even now, standing here, I still get that nauseous, stomach-churning sensation I got every day when I was let out of the carpool and had to walk up the driveway to that back door.*

He removed his left hand from his pocket, gripped the book in his right hand more tightly, took a deep breath, and began confidently walking up the driveway.

This time, he thought, *I'm not going to that back door.*

He walked up the front steps and rang the doorbell.

CHAPTER 30
Mission Accomplished

Almost instantly, the door opened, and Natalia was standing in the doorway. She screamed and lunged at Sebastian, throwing her arms around his neck and kissing his cheeks.

Finally, Natalia stepped back, holding her brother at arm's length, looking him up and down. "You look so handsome. And thin, oh, my gosh, you are so thin!" She led him into the house and closed the door. "What are you doing here? How long are you staying? Where are your bags?"

Sebastian frowned. "I think I should ask you the same thing. What are you doing here, Nat? Is everything okay?"

"Sure, everything is fine. I usually come by once a week to see Mom and Dad since I'm the only one of us who still lives in town." She looked him up and down again. "It's been a long time, Seabass."

She smiled broadly, calling him by his childhood nickname, and Sebastian smiled back.

"Really," she said, "why are you here after all these years? Why didn't you tell me you were coming the last time we talked?"

Before he could answer, Sebastian heard his mother's voice. "Natalia, what is all that noise about?" When Mrs. Warwick saw her son, her shoulders began to shake and she began to sob. "Sebastian . . .

is that really you?" she managed to say.

"Yes, Mother, it's really me." He saw that his mother still had that look of grace she'd always possessed when he was younger. He walked toward her and lightly embraced her as if he were afraid she wouldn't allow him to touch her.

As soon as his arms encircled her, she captured him in her embrace. "Oh, my baby. My baby, where have you been? I've missed you so much."

"Can't a man get some peace and quiet in his own house? Why are you making . . ." Sebastian's father entered the hall from his den. When he looked at the people standing in the hallway, he stopped short.

No one said anything for several moments, and then Nathaniel Warwick pulled his shoulders back, stood up to his full height, and folded his arms across his chest. Looking at his youngest child from head to toe, he said, "So, you've finally come back. And just look at you. Your hair is long and uncombed, and you are so thin. What happened? Are you living on the street? Don't think you are going to move back in here and live off of me again. You need to just go right back to wherever you've been all these years."

Before Sebastian could answer, Natalia stepped toward her father. "Dad, what's wrong with you? Why would you say such things to Sebastian?"

Sebastian touched his sister on the arm. "It's okay, Nat, you don't have to take up for me anymore. I can handle this now. And to answer your question," Sebastian said, looking at his father, "I'm here to clear the air between us."

"Sebastian," Mrs. Warwick said, "don't be disrespectful to your father, please."

Sebastian looked at his mother and offered her a sad smile. "Mother, you know that I love you, but some things have to be said, and I'm going to say what I've come to say. Then I will never come back here again. You, of course, will always be welcomed in my home. But I'll never come back, ever."

Mr. Warwick still held his arms folded across his chest as Sebastian approached him.

"I say that out of respect for Mom," Sebastian said, "not for you. Something you never understood was that music was my passion. Since I was ten, I've strongly felt I could make a difference, and over the last few years, I've been blessed to become recognized as a rising artist in the field of classical music. I've just completed the first set of seasonal tours for the year, and the reviews have been positive. I think that following my dream has made a difference in my life."

Sebastian looked down at his mother, who was standing by his side. "Mother, I want to thank you for being so supportive of me and helping me achieve my dream." Looking back at his father, Sebastian continued. "And you, Mr. Warwick, you have never had me in your favor for anything. Even to the bitter end, you couldn't bring yourself to say something positive, encouraging, or uplifting to me. Do you even remember some of what you said to me?"

"No. No, I don't remember. But whatever I said, I meant every word."

"I didn't think that you would," Sebastian spat. "Your kind never does."

Mr. Warwick dropped his arms and glared at his son. "What do you mean my kind? What are you trying to say? Why are you even here?" He seemed to lose his breath as he took two steps toward Sebastian. "Are you angry at me because I wanted something better for you? Because I was a good father who demanded the best from my children and you couldn't live up to my expectations? Your brother and your sister followed my wishes, and they are very successful independent adults. Are you blaming me because you are the weak link in this family chain?"

"The weak link? That's a good way to put it, but I prefer to call myself the one who got away." Sebastian smiled. "And that is what's made the difference in my life."

Turning away from his father, Sebastian took his sister and his mother by the hands. He leaned forward and kissed each of them on the cheek. "I've fallen in love with someone, and I wanted her to meet my parents, my family."

Then Sebastian dropped their hands and turned again to face his father.

"And I wanted to come here to see if you had changed your mind about me," he said, "but it's obvious you haven't. So I'm going to say something to you, and then you and I will never have to see each other again."

"Really?" Mr. Warwick said with a smirk on his face. "And what would that be?"

Sebastian moved close enough to see his father become rigid, as if he were steeling himself for a blow. Standing eye to eye with his father, he said, "I forgive you. I forgive you for being verbally, emotionally, and physically abusive to me. I forgive you for being a poor example of a father and of manhood in general."

"I'm not asking for your forgiveness. So you can keep it!" Nathaniel nearly shouted.

"Mr. Warwick, I'm not doing this for you. I'm doing this for me and the woman I've fallen in love with. Because if I don't forgive you, I wouldn't be able to love her the way she deserves to be loved by her husband, and that is unconditionally. So, yes, I forgive you."

With that said, Sebastian did something he had never done in his life. He hugged his father. And even though his father didn't return the hug, Sebastian felt his father's body wilt. When he released his father from his embrace, Sebastian turned back to his mother and sister.

Natalia was crying softly. Sebastian put his arms around her. "Thanks, Nat, I love you. Don't forget to come see me." He handed her his business card. "I really want you to visit me so we can sit up all night talking like we used to. I've missed you all these years."

When Sebastian looked at his mother, his eyes were glistening. "Mom, her name is Octavia. Dr. Octavia Peterson. She's a college professor and an award-winning author. I know you'll like her. We went to high school together, and right now, she's my next-door neighbor." He gave his mother a lingering hug, kissed both her cheeks, and whispered, "I love you, Mom. Thank you for being my shining example of grace and charm in the midst of adversity."

The book he was holding when he walked into the house was now on the side table by the front door. Sebastian picked it up and handed it to his mother.

"This is a glimpse of what my life has been like over the last fifteen years." It was a photo album. She looked at the cover and touched the lettering that read *Dr. Sebastian Warwick: Master Musician, Classical Pianist, Author, and Composer.*

Before leaving his childhood home for what he considered the last time, Sebastian reached into his inside jacket pocket and pulled out an envelope. He handed it to his father and said, "This should cover the expenses, plus interest, that you incurred in relation to me while I was growing up in your house."

CHAPTER 31
What's It All About?

When Sebastian walked out of his parents' house, his sister and mother stood in the doorway and watched him walk down the driveway.

As they were getting their last look at him, Mr. Warwick looked in the envelope and pulled out a check for $500,000.

Immediately, the stubborn, inflexible, and uncompromising older man walked to the window to watch as a limousine pulled up. The driver got out of the car and opened the door for Sebastian.

There was a slight smile on Mr. Warwick's face, and he whispered, "Maybe you're not so worthless after all. Welcome to manhood, son."

When the door of the limousine was closed, Sebastian realized he had been holding his breath. He laid his head back on the headrest, closed his eyes, inhaled deeply, and slowly released a lungful of air.

During the ride, he was preoccupied with thoughts of being with Octavia again.

He had a conversation with himself about having declared his love for his next-door neighbor to his mother and sister.

Smiling broadly, he thought, *Maybe I should tell Octavia again how I feel about her and make sure she really feels the same way.*

After an hour and a half, Sebastian felt the car begin to slow down. He lifted his head and saw the tall trees that lined the street he lived on.

Instead of waiting for the driver to open the door, Sebastian exited the car on his own. He was excited and wanted to get into his house and get some things started before Octavia got home from work.

Without unpacking or even changing his clothes, Sebastian got into his car and drove to the supermarket. In an hour he was back home, the wine was being chilled, the sirloin tips were marinating, he was washing the stir fry vegetables, and the rice was in the cooker.

The last thing he did before taking a shower was write a note to Octavia and tape it to her patio door where she would see it when she was going to the pool for her daily swim.

For reasons she couldn't explain, Octavia had been overly emotional and unsettled for most of the day. She barely made it through her classes and office hours with a civil attitude. It felt like she had butterflies in her stomach, and she tried hard to keep her anxiety under control.

"What is wrong with me?" she asked herself.

Finally, she gave up trying to keep herself together and left her office thirty-five minutes early. As she was walking toward her car, someone fell into step beside her.

"Hello, Professor Peterson, how are you?"

Myrna Edwards' voice sounded chipper, and when Octavia looked at her, she saw her colleague was smiling broadly.

"Hello, Mrs. Edwards, how are you?"

"Better than you, I'm sure. You look awful. What's wrong?"

Octavia could only shake her head. "I don't know, Myrna. I can't keep my mind on anything. My stomach is tied up in knots, and I'm so nervous that all I want to do is go home and get in bed and never get out."

"Maybe you're coming down with a cold. Perhaps you're right. You should go home and get into bed. You look exhausted. You need to get some rest. Is there anything I can do for you?" After a pause, Myrna asked, "Where is your knight in shining armor? Is he back? Is the concert season over yet?"

Myrna looked so concerned that Octavia almost broke down, but she managed to choke out, "He's not back yet, and I haven't heard from him in a week."

After giving Myrna a hug, Octavia continued to her car with a heavy heart. It was all she could do to keep her composure. She missed Sebastian, and because she hadn't heard from him in a week, she was beginning to think outrageous thoughts.

He probably didn't mean all those things he said to me and is trying to figure out a way to take back what he said, she thought.

As she was driving, she touched the play button on her disc player and immediately her car was filled with the mesmerizing sounds of "Beauty." She let the music minister to her frayed nerves and soothe her unsettled mind.

Pulling up to her house, Octavia took her time getting out of the car. *Maybe I'll hear from Sebastian tonight. I hope things are better for him now than they were last week.* She sniffed. *Someone is cooking out tonight, and it smells pretty good.*

She walked into her kitchen directly from the garage, put her briefcase on the floor, and sat at the table. After about five minutes, she thought, *I miss Sebastian. Wonder what he's doing tonight?*

Sighing deeply, she stood and walked into the bedroom to change into her bathing suit.

I may as well get my laps in since there probably won't be a phone call tonight either.

Pulling back the drapes, Octavia saw the note taped to the sliding door. Her first thought was fleeting, and she had a brief notion it might be from Matthew. With shaking hands, she opened the door and peeled the note from the window.

Hello, Dr. Peterson.

After you finish your laps, I'll be over to pick you up. Wait for me. I'm really anxious to see you, but you are worth the wait. Now hurry and get in the pool, because after you're finished, I have a surprise for you.

S. W.

Octavia was surprised and happy. She couldn't believe he was back. Without delay, she slipped out of her robe, stepped into the dome, slid into the pool, and began moving smoothly through the water.

It felt like the longest two hours of her life getting her laps in and getting dressed to see Sebastian. She was so nervous she could hardly comb and brush her hair or find the right outfit to put on. She sat waiting for her doorbell to ring.

At last, the doorbell chimed and she ran to pull it open. Standing there, looking breathtakingly handsome, was Sebastian.

Without a second thought, Octavia stepped through the door and threw her arms around him. And without hesitation, he returned her embrace. He even lifted her up and swung her around.

They stood looking at each other, smiling warmly and tenderly. Sebastian was the first to speak.

"You need to come with me, we have quite an evening before us. But first . . ." He took her by her hand and stepped into the house, then he turned to look intently at her. "You look so amazing. More beautiful than I even remembered. And in all the time I've been gone, I've been dreaming of doing this."

Sebastian looked unfalteringly into Octavia's eyes. He closed the space between them and gently cupped her face in his large hands. He leaned down to present the woman he loved with a gentle kiss that almost immediately became intense and passionate as he moved his hands from her face and let them slowly drift down her curvy, supple frame to engage her in a full-body embrace.

Not to be outdone, Octavia slowly and surely wrapped her arms around Sebastian's body just to hold onto him so she wouldn't melt into the carpet. His kiss was surprisingly delicate and loving, and it made her want more. In fact, it made her wish it would never end.

CHAPTER 32
At Last

When Octavia was guided through the front door of Sebastian's house, she was pleased to see the beautiful black shiny grand piano in the living room.

It didn't surprise her at all that there was no other furniture in the room except an overstuffed armchair with a matching ottoman. It seemed so appropriate.

The other thing she noticed was the soft lighting throughout the house. There was a wonderful aroma in the air.

"Well, Professor, don't be shy, please come in," Sebastian said with a smile. "We have a lot to do tonight, and it all begins with that amazing meal I promised you."

The conversation during dinner was pleasant and enjoyable. Octavia found it pleasurable listening to Sebastian's recounting of his concert events. It made her feel as though she were becoming a part of his life. For the first time, she let herself relax and enjoy the position of being on a date. She had a feeling this relationship was not going to end with a betrayal.

After dinner when they were loading the dishwasher, Octavia said, "You were right. That was an amazing meal, Mr. Warwick."

"Thank you," Sebastian said, smiling. "The truth is, it's the only real meal I can cook." His admission made both of them laugh.

Then Sebastian took the dishtowel from Octavia and led her by the hand from the kitchen into his den. He invited her to take a seat on the sofa and sat beside her. He looked deeply into her eyes, lifted her hands, and kissed them both, one at a time.

"Octavia, I have to tell you something, and then I have a question that I want to ask you. Will you hear me out?"

When she slowly nodded her head, Sebastian began to tell Octavia about the dysfunctional relationship he and his father had with each other. Sebastian found it difficult to stay in one place. Looking at the tenderness and concern in Octavia's face invoked some anxiety in him. He stood and walked across the room, then continued recounting the sequence of events.

He told her he had stayed away from his parents' home for fifteen years. Then he told her he had taken her advice and faced his demons.

"Yesterday, I went to the city to my parents' house. When I got out of the car, I stood outside, looking at the place I used to consider my house of horrors. I didn't think I'd be able to make myself knock on the door. Then I thought about what you said I should do. I didn't back down. I faced my demons."

Sebastian paced the room and stopped in front of the small window. Standing there, he told Octavia about the events that had unfolded between him and his family. Finally, he shared with the woman he had fallen deeply in love with the details of his ill-fated relationship with Amara and the conclusive incident that had occurred between them just six months ago at his front door.

When he finished, Sebastian turned to look at Octavia. Seeing the tear tracks on her cheeks, he crossed the room in three strides and again taking possession of her hands, he knelt in front of her.

"The reason I'm sharing this information with you is because I'm falling deeply in love with you, and I need to clear the air and ask you one more time. Do you feel the same way about me?"

Octavia offered Sebastian a gentle smile. She accepted the tissues he held out and dabbed her eyes and cheeks. Then she leaned close to him and squeezed his hands delicately. Looking deep into his eyes, she kindheartedly said, "Sebastian Warwick, you are an amazing man, and I have tremendous respect for you."

Sebastian's throat immediately felt dry. He started to experience a little anxiety, and his breathing became erratic. He was afraid she was going to brush him off. He was terrified Octavia was going to tell him she still had feelings for that jerk Matthew Edwards.

"I don't know how to tell you how I feel about you," she continued. "There are no words I can use that will let you know I love you with my whole heart. When we are together, I feel as though we're the only two people in the world. Every time I think of you, I feel my heart beating out of control. I start smiling and can't stop. Yes, Sebastian, I believe I feel the same way you do. I'm already genuinely in love with you. I love you dearly."

Sebastian jumped up and let out a shout that seemed to rattle the walls. He pulled Octavia to her feet and wrapped her in his strong, comfortable embrace. He kissed her hungrily with seemingly endless pleasure and great satisfaction.

Breaking contact, Sebastian stepped away from Octavia. "Come on, I'm going to walk you home because if we keep this up, I'll make sure you never leave this house."

He took her by the hand and walked her out of his front door. When they stepped onto Octavia's front porch, Sebastian used her key to open the door, and they stepped inside.

He held up his hand to stop her and then walked through each room. As he was standing just outside Octavia's bedroom door, he had a sudden urge to run back to the front door, scoop her up into his arms, carry her through the door of her boudoir, and take complete possession of her.

Instead, he walked back to where he had left Octavia and gave her the key. He pulled her intimately close and kissed her passionately. Looking fondly and tenderly into her eyes, he whispered, "I love you."

Just before he stepped through the doorway, he said, "Don't forget to use the deadbolt."

CHAPTER 33
The Morning After

When Octavia awoke the next morning, she was ecstatic. Her mind was still on the enchanted evening she had spent with Sebastian the night before. She thought about his beautiful declaration of love for her. She remembered how warm and comfortable she felt in his arms when he kissed her.

The entire day, her disposition was lively, energetic, and bubbly. She was so happy that the day seemed to speed by so fast. Before she knew it, her classes were over and she was in her office.

Oh, this has been a great day, she thought to herself. *Now I'm going to use this time to get myself together.*

Octavia worked steadily and completed her lesson plans for the remainder of the week. Finally, she began to review the latest student essay assignments. She couldn't wait to get home so she could see Sebastian again. She thought this would be a good time to introduce him to her parents.

When Sebastian awoke the next morning, he was also on cloud nine. In fact, he was so happy that he began making plans to ask Octavia to marry him. He remembered how he felt after dinner when she answered his question with the most beautiful words he had ever heard: "I love you dearly." Remembering her words of love for him made his heartbeat intensify with blissful delight.

He realized just the very thought of her gave him a feeling of complete calm and satisfaction. "She makes me feel like I can do anything but fail," he said out loud. Then he threw the covers back, jumped from his bed, and ran to take a quick shower.

It was Sebastian's plan to meet Octavia in her office after her last class. He was going to ask her the question of a lifetime then take her to the jewelry store before she changed her mind . . . if her answer was yes.

The thought of being married was nothing Sebastian ever thought he would contemplate. Yet here he was, considering a permanent relationship with Octavia Peterson, someone he thought was incredible, someone he didn't have to search for because she was right next door.

He was so happy that he hurried through his morning warm-up practice, and just when he was about to go into the garage and get in the car, the front doorbell rang.

"Oh, man," he said, "who could that be?"

He considered pretending he hadn't heard the bell, but when it chimed again persistently, he walked through the house and opened the door.

"Hello, son," his mother said, smiling broadly. "How are you this morning? I hope we're not disturbing you."

Then Natalia spoke up. "Hello, little brother. We've decided to take you up on your invitation. So are you going to let us in?"

Too shocked to say anything, Sebastian stepped back and let the two ladies walk into his house. As he was closing the door, he realized that he was pleased they had taken his invitation seriously.

When he turned to face his guests, Sebastian said, "I'm so glad you're here," but he couldn't say anything else because his throat had tightened and his eyes were brimming with tears.

Judith Warwick closed the space between her and her son. She wrapped him warmly in her arms, and as she held him, she shed a few tears. She was so overjoyed that they were together again, this time in an amicable manner.

"It's alright, son. I'm so glad to be here with you. I've missed you so much."

Not to be left out, Natalia stepped close and joined the embrace. Just then, the doorbell rang again. Turning the doorknob, Sebastian found himself face to face with his father. Without a word, Sebastian began to close the door in his father's face.

"Sebastian, wait," Natalia said. "Dad has something that he wants to say to you. Don't you, Dad?"

Nathaniel cleared his throat. "I know I'm the last person you thought you would ever see at your front door, but I would appreciate it if you let me speak with you before you close the door in my face."

CHAPTER 34
Face to Face

Sebastian was fighting the urge to slam the door in his father's face, but he made the mistake of looking at his mother and saw the silent pleading in her eyes. He held the door ajar and allowed his father to step through the slight opening. Then he closed the door.

Mr. Warwick looked around the room. Then he looked at his son. "Uh, is there somewhere we can talk privately?"

Still not wanting to be civil, Sebastian said nothing until his mother touched his arm. "Do you have a den, son? I think that would be a good place for you two to talk and straighten things out. Don't you agree?"

Not looking at his father, Sebastian turned and walked out of the living room. As he was leaving the room, he said, "It's because I love and respect my mother that I'm even giving you this consideration, Mr. Warwick, so let's make this quick."

Once in the den, the stoic father and the angry son stood facing each other. Then Nathaniel spoke. "Sebastian, there are some things you should know. First, I don't need, nor do I want, your money."

With that said, he handed his son the envelope that contained the certified check.

"Secondly," Mr. Warwick continued, "those things you claim I did to you that you think were so horrible and make me look like a monster . . . you need to know that it was the only way I knew how to treat you. It was the way I was raised, and it didn't seem to have harmed me. As a matter of fact, it doesn't seem that your brother had any problems with my methods of parenting. He is doing very well. Do you know that he's just opened another store? He has three of them now. I guess you could call him a successful entrepreneur. I'm really very proud of him."

Sebastian glared at his father. "Do you realize that Nate Jr. is working on his third marriage? Don't you think that perhaps his not being able to sustain a long-term relationship is evidence of having some problems?"

"There's nothing wrong with your brother other than he hasn't found the right woman yet."

Sebastian walked across the room and sat at his desk. "I have rages! I have episodes when I get so angry that I just want to destroy something."

"And you're blaming that on me? You were never able to live up to my expectations, and you want to blame me for your lack of fortitude?"

"No, I'm not blaming you for anything. Because you believe yourself to be among the select few in this world who has never done anything wrong. You need to understand something. I long ago stopped caring about your opinion of me. Your way of thinking has no consideration in my life."

Sebastian looked critically at his father and saw he was looking his age, maybe a few years beyond. But because he had no attachment to the man at all, Sebastian matter-of-factly continued with his statement.

"I just want to know why you never accepted me as your son. It seemed that whatever Nate Jr. did was great and whatever I did was always unacceptable. Even if I did the same things he did, you constantly found fault with me and everything that I did."

Mr. Warwick glared at his son. Then he took a deep breath and forcefully spat out, "Because for a long time, I didn't think that you were my son!"

He looked away and walked to the small corner window. Neither man spoke for a few moments.

Nathaniel Warwick, at length, went on. "The year you were born, your mother and I were having problems. She took your brother and sister and left me. When she returned, she was obviously pregnant. She insisted it was my baby, but I never believed her.

"It wasn't until you were seventeen and I needed a blood transfusion and you were the only family member that was a true match. That was when I was forced to accept you were my son. But by that time, I was so tied up in my own fear about dying and leaving my family behind that I didn't take the time to think more positively about you.

"Besides, you were so different from my idea of a son that I couldn't accept you for who you were. I just didn't know how to rectify the situation. It was easier to keep things the way they had always been rather than to take the time to make a change."

Sebastian was stunned. He couldn't believe what he had just heard. He rose from his chair, crossed the room, and stood over his father. The old man looked small and powerless.

With deliberation and barely controlled anger, Sebastian asked, "Are you . . . for real? Did you really just say . . ."

He couldn't finish the question. He couldn't quite take in everything his father had just said to him.

When his father would not make eye contact and made no attempt to verify what he had just revealed as truth, Sebastian turned and quickly exited the den. He didn't stop to talk to his mother or his sister; he just stalked through the kitchen and into the garage. He hardly waited for the door to lift before he propelled the car out of the enclosure and raced down the quiet, deserted street.

CHAPTER 35
Setting Things in Order

As she was leaving her office, Octavia felt as though she were walking on air and that her feet were hardly touching the ground. She couldn't remember the last time she had felt this happy and carefree.

"What are you so happy about?" a voice said. She recognized it immediately as Matthew's.

"Hello, Matthew," she said, "how are you today?" She did not break her stride, but Matthew nonetheless fell in step beside her. "Go away. We have nothing to talk about."

"On the contrary, Professor, we have a lot to talk about," he countered. "I know you still have some feelings for me. I know I'm not that forgettable. At least not to someone like you, anyway."

Octavia stopped abruptly and looked at Matthew. He had a smug look on his face. She smiled and thought, *He is so unrightfully full of himself. What a jerk!*

"Matthew, you have some nerve. How dare you think I could have any kind of feelings for the likes of you? You are so pathetic. The only thing I feel for you is disgust and pity. You have so much to be grateful for, and here you are throwing all of that away just to feed your ego."

She folded her arms across her chest and looked him up and down.

"You have a beautiful, intelligent wife, and I'm sure your children are delightful, intelligent, and well behaved. But obviously that's not enough for you because here you are, trying to score. You need help."

Then Octavia dropped her arms and stared into Matthew's face. "You're a pathetic little person who thinks more of himself than he should. You're so foolish. You've been blessed beyond measure and you don't even know it. Get away from me and don't ever speak to me again or I'll report you to the dean and you'll lose this position, too. And this time when you leave for another job, I'm sure you'll probably be leaving alone."

Octavia saw that she had struck a nerve with one Matthew Edwards. He stood glaring at her with his mouth open as though he were trying to catch his breath.

She pursed her lips. "Uh-huh, just as I thought. Nothing but a big old windbag. You're so full of yourself. It makes me sick thinking I almost fell for your smooth line and empty emotional drivel."

She shook her head and continued her verbal assault. "Matthew Edwards, you've gotten on my last good nerve. Get out of my face, and if we ever find ourselves in each other's presence, let's pretend that we're disinterested strangers. As a matter of fact, if I see you first, I promise I'll turn around and go in the opposite direction so we don't have to go through the pretense."

Because she couldn't stand to look at him anymore, Octavia turned and walked resolutely to her car. When she finally made it, she whispered, "Thank you, Lord, for showing me that a relationship with Matthew Edwards would have been more than a mistake."

As she drove, she thought that she must have looked insane to people in other cars. She was driving alone, smiling broadly.

I bet those people think I'm off my rocker. If they only knew, they'd understand why I can't stop beaming like a ray of sunshine. I'm crazy, alright . . . crazy in love with that fine, sexy Sebastian Warwick.

She drove straight to Mom and Pop Harrington's and picked them up, then turned her car toward home.

She was eager to see Sebastian and to have him meet the Harringtons.

CHAPTER 36
Meeting the Family

After two hours of driving aimlessly, Sebastian stopped his car on a street a few miles from his house. He was parked in an area that overlooked the residential buildings on the university campus. For a while, he sat looking across the beautiful, colorful horizon.

Eventually, he exited his car and sat on the hood. He took out his cell phone and looked at the calls he had ignored. There were four from his sister, and Octavia had called twice. He listened to Natalia's messages then quickly dialed Octavia's number. When she answered, her voice was like a balm. It soothed him and eased some of the pain that had gripped his heart.

"Hello, Sebastian, where are you? I'd like for you to come meet my parents tonight. Would you come over at seven?"

Sebastian looked at his watch. He had an hour and forty-five minutes before he would see her. He wondered if he could hold it together that long. He closed his eyes and reclined on the windshield of his car.

"Hello yourself, Miss Peterson. How are you today?" It was so good to hear her voice. "Of course I'll be at your house, but I have some guests at my house, and I'd like you to meet them. Do you mind if I bring some company?"

When he turned his car onto his street, Sebastian noticed his parents' car was no longer in the driveway. "They must have left," he said to himself. He didn't know why, but he felt disappointed.

When he went inside, he found his mother sitting at the kitchen table. There were several pots on the stove, and the house smelled like fresh cornbread, roast beef, garlic potatoes, and broccoli.

"Why are you cooking?" he asked. "You didn't have to do that, you know."

Judith looked at her son. She got up and walked across the room to stand in front of her tall, handsome child. "You've been through a lot today. Why don't you go change so you can relax, and we can have one of your favorite home-cooked meals."

"We've been invited to dinner by Octavia next door. I'd like you to meet her."

Just then, Natalia walked into the kitchen. After giving her brother a light punch on the shoulder, she said, "Now I remember who she is. She's that chunky girl you went to high school with."

"Oh, be quiet, Nat," Sebastian said. "She's not overweight anymore. Besides, it wouldn't matter to me if she were."

"I believe that my baby brother is blinded by love," Natalia said.

The trio laughed, and it seemed the air in the room became lighter. When they settled down, Sebastian looked around the kitchen and even stepped into his living room.

Curious, he asked, "Where is he? Did he go back home?"

Judith promptly said, "Just after you drove away, your father got in the car and took off in the opposite direction."

"Let's take the food over to Octavia's house and have dinner there," Sebastian suggested, and the women agreed.

Just as they were setting the meat on a platter and putting the vegetables into bowls, Nathaniel Warwick returned.

"Daddy," Natalia said, "we've been invited to dinner by Sebastian's next-door neighbor."

Before Nathaniel could make a disagreeable remark, his wife stepped to him, looked into his eyes, and said very quietly through gritted teeth and pursed lips, "Nate, we are going, and you will behave in a most respectful manner, or I will carry out my promise. Now go freshen up and be quick about it!"

Octavia and the Harringtons were in her kitchen, working on dinner. Mom was checking on the deep-dish lasagna in the oven. Pop Harrington was lavishly spreading garlic butter on loaves of French bread, and Octavia was preparing a salad.

"Mom, Dad, I can hardly wait for Sebastian to get here. I know that you're simply going to love this man. He's just so . . . ."

She didn't finish. When she heard the lock on the gate disengage, Octavia's heart began to pound. She ran to open the back door. She was taken aback when she saw Sebastian with two beautiful women and a man with a sour look on his face. By the look on Sebastian's face, it seemed he wanted to do harm to something or somebody.

Octavia welcomed everyone, invited them into the kitchen, and made a quick group introduction of her parents and herself. Sebastian stepped forward and introduced himself and his family.

"Dr. and Mrs. Harrington, I'm Sebastian Warwick. This is my mother, Judith, my sister, Natalia, and my fa . . . this is . . . Nathaniel Warwick."

Sensing the tension, the Harringtons stepped forward and spoke to each member of the Warwick family. Pop Harrington asked Nathaniel to join him in the den to check on the current football game while Mom Harrington invited the ladies into the kitchen.

"I see you've brought over some delicious-smelling dishes," she said. "Let's get that food warmed up so we can sit down at the table and get acquainted with each other."

As the evening progressed, everyone seemed to enjoy getting to know one another. Mrs. Warwick and Mrs. Harrington found they both loved collecting recipes and trying their hands at cooking new dishes. Mr. Warwick and Dr. Harrington found they had mutual interests in sports and politics. Octavia and Natalia found they both loved reading the classics and spent time during dinner discussing their favorite books and authors.

Through all of the friendship building, Sebastian spent the evening on the outskirts of the conversations. Octavia noticed and tried several times to make eye contact with him, but he appeared determined to be detached and uninvolved.

After the meal was finished and the dessert had been served, the two older men returned to the den, each carrying a mug brimming with steaming coffee. While the rest of the ladies cleared the table, Octavia finally got the opportunity to spend some time alone with Sebastian.

She led him to the living room, and when they were out of sight of everyone, she turned to him and slid her arms around his waist. It took a few moments for him to return the embrace, and when he did, it was intense.

As they were standing together, he whispered to her, "I've been waiting all day to get you in my arms. I've needed to feel your warm, loving tenderness. I love you, Octavia Peterson." With that said, he kissed her gently and affectionately. "Go back into the kitchen. I have to go home. I didn't get a chance to do my afternoon practice today, and I need to do that. I'll be back to ride with you when you take the Harringtons home."

Smiling, Octavia dropped her arms and stood back. When she looked into Sebastian's beautiful black eyes, she couldn't see the peaceful composure that was usually there. Instead of addressing it, she leaned forward, reached up, cupped his face in her hands, and kissed his cheek.

"I would love to have you ride with me, now go home. I want to hear your hands gliding across those keys, making beautiful music like only you can."

When he held out his hand, she took it and let him lead her through the front door, across the porch to the steps.

"Thanks again for everything," he said. "It was a pleasure to meet Dr. and Mrs. Harrington. Now go back inside. I'll see you in a little while."

As she watched him walk across the lawn, she noticed there was no rhythm in his step, and his shoulders drooped. "Whatever it is, my love," she whispered, "I pray that you let God work it out for you."

Before she turned to step back inside, she wiped the tears from her cheeks.

CHAPTER 37
Talent Revealed

The ladies in the kitchen stopped what they were doing. They stood perfectly still as if their movement would stop the flow of beautiful music coming from Sebastian's house.

Natalia was the first to speak. "Oh, my goodness, he is such a gifted musician. That music is so beautiful."

Judith spoke next. "It's so enchanting and delicate. What is the name of that piece?"

From the doorway, through a new round of tears, Octavia said, "It's called 'Beauty' and he said he composed it for me . . . even though he didn't know me at the time."

Mom Harrington put down the dishtowel and walked over to her daughter. When she spread her arms, Octavia stepped into her motherly embrace.

"Mom, there's something wrong, and he hasn't said anything. He keeps his feelings inside, and then he locks himself in that house and plays the piano for hours. He's hurting, and I can't do anything about it."

Nathaniel Warwick walked into the kitchen to get a refill of coffee and stopped short when he saw the four ladies standing in the middle of the room, crying on each other's shoulders. "What is this?" he asked. "What is going on? For heaven's sake, what is wrong now?"

Judith looked at him and said, "Nathaniel, just listen, please!"

He did. After a few moments, he set his cup on the kitchen table and walked out the back door. Quietly, he slipped into his son's house and stood in the kitchen. Humbly and respectfully, he listened to his son playing the most beautiful music he had ever heard.

At that moment, Nathaniel Warwick felt a burden of regret settle in his chest. His body became so laden with guilt and shame that he had to lean against the counter to prevent from falling to the floor. As the music continued, the callous, harsh, unwavering older man let himself get lost in the musical talent his son was displaying.

He was genuinely astounded that Sebastian was so artistically gifted.

Begrudgingly, he admitted to himself, *Up to this point in time, it was beyond my wildest notions that he could have ever become successful at anything. But here I am, standing in his home, listening to him play so brilliantly.* Then he straightened his shoulders, stood up straight, and whispered, "Hmm, that's amazing."

Nathaniel turned and slowly exited his son's residence, returning to the house next door. When he went inside, he saw that Brad Harrington had joined the ladies in the kitchen. The five of them were all seated at the table with glasses of lemonade and mugs of coffee in front of them. They all seemed to be enjoying the concert, so Nathaniel refilled his coffee cup and joined them.

The free concert lasted an hour and a half. The audience was so mesmerized that no one spoke or even moved while Sebastian played out his deepest feelings.

When the music stopped, Pop Harrington spoke softly to the group, "If that was a practice session, can you just imagine how powerful the actual concert must be?"

Judith took a deep breath and gently said, "I can't believe how magnificent his playing has become."

Nathaniel leaned forward and asked his wife, "What do you mean . . . has become? You knew that he had talent?"

Judith looked at her husband and, in a severely critical voice, said, "Of course I knew he was talented. He did, after all, receive a full ride to Julliard, didn't he?"

The atmosphere in Octavia's kitchen became tense. For a few moments, no one spoke. Finally, Natalia ended the silence. "Oh, yes, that's my little brother! I'm so proud of him."

"He is such an amazing person," Octavia added. "Being a master musician is just one part of who he is."

Mom Harrington wrapped Octavia in a motherly hug and whispered in her ear, "Congratulations, sweetie, you're in love."

Just then, there was a light knock on the door. When Sebastian stepped through the threshold, he was taken aback to see everyone sitting in the kitchen and looking at him with such a myriad of expressions on their faces.

All at once, everyone stood and began clapping. Natalia stood and hugged him. "Little brother, we were all sitting here enjoying your playing. It was beautiful!"

Everyone began to speak at the same time. Then, not knowing what more to do to add to the moment, Nathaniel simply stepped to his son, patted him on the shoulder, and exited the room quietly.

CHAPTER 38
Reconciliation

Sebastian gave his family members beds for the night. Then he went with Octavia to deliver the Harringtons to their home. As they pulled back into Octavia's driveway and through the open garage door, Sebastian said, "I think I owe you an explanation for my attitude today."

For the next hour, the couple sat in the car inside the garage as Sebastian shared the conversation he'd had with his father.

"I was headed out to meet you this afternoon when they arrived," Sebastian said, "and I didn't know what to think when he asked if we could talk. That's when he finally admitted that he had never accepted me as his son."

"How do you feel about it?" Octavia asked.

Sebastian was quiet for a while, then he said, "I'm glad he finally said something. I still don't like him, but at least I know why he treated me like he did. So now I can release all of that anger and bitterness I had toward him. I'll probably never forget some of what he's said and done, but at least now I feel there's closure to that part of my life. I'm free. And because I don't ever want to feel like a despicable wretch again, I need to replace those old feelings and emotions with something new."

Octavia looked at him and smiled. "And just what is that something new?"

Sebastian opened the car door, walked around to the passenger side of the vehicle, and helped her to stand. He smiled. "I'm replacing that old hatred and anger with contentment, true happiness, love, and passion."

Then, slowly and deliberately, he wrapped his arms around Octavia and kissed her until they were both weak.

The contact was so powerful that even after the kiss ended, they had to hold on to each other. Sebastian held Octavia until his heart slowed down. When she felt his arms gather her closer to his body, Octavia was so relieved that she leaned on Sebastian's chest and held on so she wouldn't faint. She was so happy that she felt lightheaded.

Sebastian wanted to let her know he considered their relationship to be a serious one. So he said, "Octavia, I know we've only been reacquainted with each other for a few months now, but I think we were destined to be a couple. When we're together, I feel complete. You give me an emotional security I've never felt with anyone else."

Then he stepped back and took a deep breath. "This is not where I thought it would happen, but . . . Octavia Peterson, will you marry me?"

Without hesitation, Octavia whispered, "Yes, Sebastian Warwick, I would be happy to marry you."

Hugging her comfortably, Sebastian whispered, "I love you."

Later that night in bed, Octavia's mind was in a whirl. Tonight she had no music to lull her to sleep, but it didn't matter. She didn't think she could have fallen asleep right away anyway. She was so happy that she could hardly keep from screaming and jumping up and down.

After Sebastian had secured Octavia in her house, he walked into his kitchen through the back door where Natalia sat waiting for him. "I made some tea, Seabass. Do you want a cup?" she asked.

"No," he said, "but I want you to congratulate me. I just asked Octavia to marry me, and she said yes." Then he put his finger to his lips to shush her and whispered, "I don't want to tell Mom until tomorrow. As a matter of fact, I want to tell her and the Harringtons at the same time when we all get back together."

Natalia silently congratulated her brother with a broad smile, a pat on the shoulder, and a kiss on the cheek. The siblings bade each other good night and went to their beds.

It was early the next morning when Octavia's phone rang. Stepping out of the shower, she ran to snatch the receiver from the cradle. "Hello?" she answered, sounding out of breath.

"Good morning, are you alright?" Sebastian asked. "You sound out of breath."

Octavia enjoyed hearing the happiness in his voice. "I was in the shower, but I knew it was you and I didn't want to miss your call."

They talked while she dressed for work, and later when she backed her car out of the garage, Sebastian was standing in the driveway. He walked to her side of the car, opened the door, leaned in, gave her a dazzling smile, and kissed her until her lips were puffy.

"I'm going to meet you right here after work," he said. "We're going to your parents' house to let them know you're going to be mine from here on out." He leaned in for another kiss. "Now, you get going. Have a wonderful day, and I'll see you after work."

"You are certainly in a great mood for this time of day," Octavia said, but he wasn't the only one. In spite of being a little fatigued from lack of sleep, she felt pretty cheery and joyful herself.

Smiling as she backed her car onto the street, Octavia looked at the tall, well-assembled man standing in her driveway and said aloud to herself, "Yes, Mom, I really do love him."

CHAPTER 39
I'm Satisfied

Sebastian walked up his driveway and through the passageway into his back yard. Opening the small side gate, he stopped short when he saw his father sitting on the patio.

"It's a little too cool to be sitting here," Sebastian said. "Don't you want to go inside?"

"No, uh, s-s-s. I, uh . . . I just wanted to have a talk with you if you don't mind."

Sebastian stepped past him to turn on the gas-powered heater and sat across the table facing his father.

Nathaniel took in a deep breath. "I never had a kind word from my father, and so I didn't know how to treat you any differently. And for that, son, I am truly sorry. I would like for us to get to know each other if that's at all possible."

Sebastian's face was set in a frown with his forehead furrowed and his lips pressed into a thin line. This was the first time he could remember his father addressing him directly and especially using the word "son."

"Um, I guess we could at least try," Sebastian said.

They sat on the patio for a while, much to the pleasure of Judith. She and her husband had had a serious conversation well into the night, and for only the second time in their forty-five-year marriage, she had chosen to uncompromisingly demand that he respect her wishes.

She had finished their late-night conversation with a promise. "If you don't do this, Nathaniel, rest assured that you will be returning home without me, and I will never spend time in your presence again!"

It appeared Nathaniel had taken his wife's word of warning to heart, and he was trying to repair a seriously damaged if not destroyed relationship with his youngest child.

As she watched the two men, Judith offered a prayer. "Dear Lord, soften my child's heart so that he can accept his father's apology, and allow them to build a mutual respect for one another."

She was so intent that she didn't hear Natalia come into the kitchen. "Mom, what are you looking at?"

Judith smiled at her daughter and beckoned her to come look out the window. "Isn't that a beautiful sight?" she said.

By the time Sebastian and Nathaniel entered the kitchen, Judith and Natalia had prepared a beautiful breakfast.

"Mom, this looks good," Sebastian said, "but I have to finish my morning practice session before I have anything to eat, or I'll get lazy." As he was walking through the kitchen, he said, "You all enjoy, but be sure to save me some steak, biscuits, and eggs so I can make a sandwich after practice!"

For only the second time as a unit, the Warwick family sat and listened to their son and little brother play the piano in his most remarkable manner.

Later in the afternoon, Sebastian was sitting in his office when Natalia walked in and closed the door behind her. She sat on the loveseat across from Sebastian's desk. "Bass, do you love this girl, or are you lonely? Because you know you don't have to get married. You can just be neighbors with benefits."

Sebastian looked at her like she was speaking a foreign language. "Nat, what did you say? Are you serious?" He stood, walked around his desk, and sat next to Natalia. "Octavia is an amazing woman, and I can't disrespect her like that. She deserves to be treated with the highest regard. I love her, Nat."

"Yeah, but you haven't known her for very long, and you think you love her? Are you sexually compatible? Is she financially stable? There's a lot you don't know about her. I think you're rushing it. Why?"

Sebastian couldn't believe what he was hearing. He took a deep breath and slowly released it. He walked over to the window and leaned his shoulder against the frame.

"Octavia and I have known each other since high school." His eyes took on a distant look, and when he spoke, there was a melancholy tone in his voice. "She was the girl everyone at school picked on when they weren't picking on me. She grew up as a ward of the state, and from the time she was three years old until she was eighteen, she was in seven foster homes. She told me it was on her eighteenth birthday that she was dropped by the state and was literally put out on the street to fend for herself."

He pushed away from the window frame.

"Nat, she had enough fortitude to get into college and make a decent life for herself in spite of her rough and unconventional childhood."

Not acknowledging the tightness in his chest and the sadness in his heart, Sebastian fixed a broad smile on his face.

"Here's what I know about her. Octavia is a genuine person, and she is remarkably stable in spite of all that she's been through in her life. And at this point, I know all I need to know about her."

Natalia looked at her brother and stood. She walked across the room and rested her hands on his shoulders, looked up at him, and smiled.

When he realized his sister had nothing to say, he returned her smile. "So I guess you want an answer to your questions, huh? Well, we haven't been intimate yet, so I don't know about the compatible part, but I think that's what the honeymoon is all about, isn't that so? And I believe a woman her age who has earned a Ph.D., teaches college, is a published poet, an award-winning novelist, and owns her own home must be fairly financially stable. So what else you got, big sister?"

Natalia couldn't help but return his broad smile with one of her own. "Okay, Seabass, I think I can step back on this one. You seem pretty sure of yourself and of Dr. Octavia Peterson." She gave him a quick hug and walked out of the den.

Before she closed the door, Sebastian called to her, "Nat, tell Mom I said not to worry." When she turned back to him, he smiled. "You didn't fool me for a minute. I knew you were on a mission for Judith Warwick, the protective mom."

As the door closed between them, each heard the other laugh quietly.

CHAPTER 40
Being Extravagant

It was a delightful day for Octavia even though she was at work, not just because it was her one-class and one-office-hour day, but because she would see Sebastian earlier than usual. She had gotten through her lecture and office hour without any complications, and now she was ready to go home and see how things had progressed with Sebastian and his family.

As she got closer to her car, Octavia thought of something that made her laugh. By the time she got into her car, she had made up her mind that she was finally going to do something impulsive—something she hadn't done in years. Instead of going straight home, she detoured through the city to a small mall she had heard about. It was a boutiques mall, and she stopped in several of the shops.

When she got home, her arms were loaded with little purchases that could have been called indulgences . . . because they were. She had a bottle of intoxicating perfume, some bath salts, and body butter that accentuated the delicate scent of the perfume. Her other purchases included a pair of shimmering drop earrings, a black pantsuit designed to emphasize her full curves, and new makeup, including glittering mascara, sparkling lip rouge, and a professionally selected foundation.

As a final act of extravagance, Octavia had even gotten a full manicure and pedicure with matching polish and nail designs so that the open-toed shoes she'd purchased would look enchanting in her new suit.

And because she wanted to feel feminine, Octavia's final luxury was a personal one no one but her would know about: three sets of lace foundation teddies, one red, one black, and one lavender. She had never indulged herself like this before, but she didn't care. She'd never been proposed to before. She was feeling happy and carefree, and she wanted to look that way.

Octavia saw Sebastian sitting on her front steps when she turned onto her street. His face lit up when he recognized her car. As she drove into her driveway, he stood and walked to the garage door, and when she pulled in and turned off the engine, he reached in, helped her from the car, and kissed her slowly and affectionately.

"Where have you been?" he asked. "I've been waiting for you."

"Well, I'll put it this way," Octavia said, smiling, "I'm so overjoyed with the prospect of being your wife that I stepped outside my box and treated myself to a few luxuries." Then she reached into the car, grabbed her bags, and invited him in to see what she had bought.

As they were going through the bags—all except one—Sebastian began to smile. "You must have been reading my mind. I made reservations at Camille's for 7:45 tonight and everyone will be there, so get dressed and I'll pick you up in an hour."

He gave her a quick kiss. Just as he was leaving, he turned back with a sly, secretive smile. "Wear the lavender one. I imagine it would look very sexy on you."

Octavia gasped and covered her face with both hands. Sebastian chuckled and closed the door.

As their party entered the restaurant, the host recognized Sebastian. "Welcome to our restaurant, Mr. Sebastian. It's an honor to have you and your party dine with us this evening."

Just as they were being seated, the owner walked over and welcomed him again, then asked, "Mr. Warwick, would you mind posing for a picture by our piano so that we can hang it on our wall of fame?"

Sebastian looked at the man and offered, "If I pose for you, you'll have to pay an entertainment fee, but I think I have some publicity shots in my trunk. I'll give you one, then you can hang that, and everyone will be happy."

When Sebastian and the man exited the restaurant, Nathaniel said, "Is he crazy? He just cut himself out of probably a nice piece of money."

Brad said, "I don't think it's about the money with your son. I think it's about the appreciation and respect for his fans."

Nathaniel made no comment but seemed to acknowledge and respect the assumption his new friend offered. When the musician and the restaurateur returned, they were both smiling.

"To thank you for your kindness," the owner said, "I would like for you and your party to dine in our private dining room tonight."

Nathaniel leaned toward Brad. "Well, all of a sudden, Dr. Harrington, I believe I can see what you're talking about. This is a simple case of one hand washing the other." Both men smiled and nodded their heads in agreement.

The Warwick party was relocated to a beautiful room with floor to ceiling windows and several stained-glass skylights in the ceiling. There was a magnificent view of the city through each window, and the late-evening sun was shining through the stained glass, making brilliant colors like a kaleidoscope around the room.

CHAPTER 41
All in Agreement

"This seems as good a time as any to tell them all our good news," Sebastian said, smiling at Octavia.

She looked at him affectionately and squeezed his hand lightly.

"Excuse me, everyone," Sebastian said. He looked across the table and winked at his mother. "Dr. and Mrs. Harrington, I want to tell you that your daughter and I have been dating for over six months, and last night I asked her to be my wife. But before we can be officially engaged, I have to ask if you would give me your consent to court your beautiful daughter and your permission to marry her."

Octavia stood and leaned toward Sebastian until their shoulders touched. All eyes were on the couple. No one made a move or said a word for several moments. It seemed the family members were stunned.

Pop Harrington pushed back his chair. "You know, young man, Octavia is very precious to us, and we want her to be happy. So I want to ask the two of you to take your time. Don't rush into something you may not be ready for."

Sebastian was a little taken aback; he didn't know what to say. Then Octavia spoke up. "Pop, we're not planning to get married tomorrow. We're going to be engaged for a while."

Judith stood and lifted her glass. "Son, I like Octavia, and I know she loves you. I believe you two will be very happy together. So whenever it is that you plan to marry, I want you to know I have no objections."

She turned and looked at the other people at the table. They each stood and raised their glasses and toasted the couple.

The Harringtons were all smiles. Pop Harrington said, "Of course you have our permission," and vigorously shook Sebastian's hand.

Mom Harrington looked at her daughter and said, "He's amazing, sweetheart. We wish you both many years of happiness together." Then she turned to Sebastian and hugged him. "If she loves you, then we love you too. Congratulations, son!"

For Sebastian, the most rewarding comment came from his father. Nathaniel stood slowly, and for the first time in his life, he embraced his son.

Then Nathaniel lifted his glass. "For all the wasted years, I want to apologize to you. I have a new perspective of who you are, and I want you to know I'm proud of you, son. You are quite a man."

Sebastian smiled as he and his father hugged one another again. Breaking the embrace, both men reached for Octavia and included her in their celebration.

ABOUT THE AUTHOR

G. Louise Beard was born in Baltimore, Maryland. The second of five children, she earned a B.S. in Special Education from Coppin State College. She and her family relocated to Ogden, Utah, where she earned an M.Ed. in Secondary Education from Weber State University.

An avid reader, she spent her early years dreaming of becoming a writer, however the necessities of life—marriage, raising a family, teaching, becoming a minister/pastor's wife—took priority and kept the dream at bay.

Now in retirement, she is taking advantage of the opportunity to fulfill her dream of becoming a published author.

Made in the USA
Las Vegas, NV
06 April 2021